A Different Shade of Blue

HILDIE MCQUEEN

Pink Door Publishing
Augusta, Georgia 2013

A DIFFERENT SHADE OF BLUE
SHADES OF BLUE SERIES

Copyright Hildie McQueen 2013

Pink Door Publishing
Augusta, Georgia

Second Edition, February 2016
Cover Artist: Robin Ludwig Design Inc.
Editor: Scott Moreland
Interior Formatting: Author E.M.S.

ISBN: 978-1-939356-43-7

Published in the United States of America

A Different Shade of Blue

*This book is dedicated to my awesome readers
who wait for my next release and then
write to tell me how much they enjoy the books.*

You, my friends, are better than any gift ever!

Prologue

Alder Gulch, Montana 1865

Grayson's knees sunk into the fresh, damp soil as he fell forward onto his hands with his head hanging between unsteady arms. The skies rained on his back, the soft drizzle mocking his tears. Sobs racked his lungs until he could not catch a breath, each wail followed by another. The pain that cut deep into his chest squeezed so hard he wondered if death would come and claim him, too. It would be a welcome reprieve to the agony of losing his Sophia, to the relentless presence of absolute sorrow that encompassed him for the last three days.

Sophia was dead, he understood this on some level, but he could not stop the persistent expectation that she'd materialize, walk up to him and be puzzled by his sadness. Any minute, she'd arrive and, in her sweet way, tease him. "Whatever is the matter with you, dear? Look at me, I am fine."

Impossible. He'd never hear the musical sound of her voice, nor feel her soft touch again. His wife of only two weeks was dead and it could not be changed.

"Come on, son. Let's go back to the house. Your mother

will worry." His father's deep tones penetrated through the fog that circled his head, but Grayson did not budge. Instead, he shrugged out from under the heavy palm on his shoulder.

"No. Leave me. Please." His voice was hoarse from hours of grief. The fact his sorrow pained his parents did not matter to him in the least. If ever there was a time for him to be selfish, this was it.

Hank Cole sank onto the dirt next to him and Grayson turned his tear-streaked face away. It proved unfortunate when a small bunch of wilted flowers caught his eye. Blue Astor, Sophia liked them, kept them in a cup on their night table.

With a loud groan, Grayson threw himself onto the grave and began to pound his fists into the dirt. "No! No! Oh God. Why?"

He didn't know how much time passed with him lying on the dirt, crying, not accepting the truth, his face caked in mud, a mixture of earth and tears.

The sun descended and temperatures cooled. Sophia did not care for the dark and now she lay under the mound of dirt in the blackness. Every night she'd be out here alone.

"I'll stay out here tonight, Pa," Grayson spoke for the first time in hours, his voice more like a croak.

"No, you will not. Grayson get up. You have to let her rest." The angry edge to his father's voice snapped him out of the haze and he began to shake uncontrollably.

"Too soon...I can't leave her out here alone. Don't you understand?"

"You know I do." His father's quiet reply made him squeeze his swollen eyes shut.

"I'm sorry, Pa."

"Don't apologize. My mother was old and it was time for her to pass. I understand. This is different. Young people are not supposed to die. A young bride is not supposed to be snatched from her husband after only two weeks. It's not right."

Grayson lifted his gaze to his father. "What am I going to do?" Pain tore a fiery path across his lungs and his breathing became labored. Steady, thick arms surrounded him and he allowed himself to collapse against his father's sturdy frame. Not able to stop them, once again the heavy tears poured.

"Just what you're doing. Son, mourn her loss and cry. A little less every day until you're done."

The sun set below the horizon and his father remained until late into the night, holding Grayson while he attempted to accept that his wife was gone. Torn from him by a careless, faceless death.

Chapter One

Five Years Later.

The dark paneled walls of their dining room did little to help the dimness of the lanterns strategically placed on the sideboard and center of the table. The thick draperies allowed for a precious few rays of the outdoor light to trickle in. Nora Banks ate the flavorful stew, attempting to ignore her mother's pointed look. Her father, at the head of the table, ate without looking up, while her brother, Mitch, sat at across from her, his spoon moving nonstop from his mouth to the bowl.

The topic of conversation was most uncomfortable for everyone, except the matron who exhaled loudly and continued on with her familiar ramblings. "I'll never see the sweet face of my grandchildren. Much longer and I'll have one foot in the grave before they are even born. Honestly, I don't understand what you two have against marriage and family life."

Her father patted his wife's hand and attempted to change the topic. "There, there, dear. Did I tell you the yellow calico you've been waiting for finally arrived?" As always, her father steered the conversation to their mercantile business.

Ignoring her husband, Carolyn Banks continued unabated. "So it seems that Lily Peters is expecting her second child. Lord, she's only been married a bit over two years. Her mother is as proud as a peacock, of course. It was all she spoke about at our quilting guild meeting. This is her third grandchild, as you all know. Her oldest boy and his wife have a beautiful little girl."

Nora's older brother, Mitch, rolled his eyes before meeting hers and she bit back the urge to smile at him. Neither Mitch nor she had married as yet, much to their mother's mortification. "Nora, are you listening to me?"

"Yes, of course, Mother. Lily. Baby. Marriage."

"Do not make light of this, Nora Elaine Banks. It's a most serious matter. Do you want to remain a single spinster living alone in that tiny cottage of yours? No, I don't think so. You're almost twenty-six. It's silly to wait any longer. Another couple of years and you won't be able to have children. Is that what you want?"

Nora pulled at the bell sleeves of her simple, blue calico, schoolmarm frock. The lace on the end of the sleeve needed replacing, but she didn't dare bring it to her mother's attention. She'd just be lectured about preferring to teach rather than remaining at home and learning the finer arts needed of a wife.

"No, Mother, it is not what I want. But I cannot force a man to marry me." Nora kept her voice even and peeked from under her lashes to see if her mother was convinced.

Her mother's wide eyes took Nora in. "What? Goodness, of course you cannot force a man to marry you. However, you have options, young lady. For goodness sakes, if you'd just accept Bronson Cole's courtship. The boy has gone so far as to speak to your father and ask for permission to court you with intentions of marriage. Why won't you accept him?"

Nora kept her eyes on her plate. Her mother's question was not an easy one to answer. The reason for her aversion to a courtship with Bronson Cole was something she could not explain. Not to her parents. And not to Bronson. No, she couldn't disclose the truth to anyone, ever.

"This pie is delicious!" Mitch spoke up and Nora shot him a thankful look. "Can I have another slice, Mother?"

"No, Mitchell, you may not have any more pie. You, too, are almost past the age to marry. What in the world is keeping you from seeking Olivia Dougherty as a wife? Her mother told me you've called on her more than once this week."

A strangle noise rose from Mitch's throat, followed by hard coughing. He turned a dreadful shade of red while his eyes bulged from the exertion. Nora jumped from her chair and rounded her brother. Her palm flat, she slapped his back in quick succession until he stopped hacking.

Her father, ever patient, took his wife's hands in his and stood. "Let's go out for some air, dear. You're becoming very upset. Come, I'll sit with you on the front porch." The rustling of her mother's skirts followed by the scraping of the chair against the wooden floor preceded her father helping his wife up. Hand in hand, their parents walked out, but not before their mother shot a look over her shoulder at them. The matter was definitely not over.

Mitch reached for the pie plate and scooped the last slice onto his plate. "Perhaps you should consider Mother's advice, Nora."

The light from the lantern on the table threw shadows at her brother's face when he leaned forward and speared a large piece of pie with his fork and ate it. A smile curved her lips and she reached for his plate, slid it closer and plunged her fork into the crust. Lifting the trophy to her mouth, she watched Mitch follow his lost prize closely. "I cannot marry Bronson Cole. You know that better than anyone. I can never marry, not without having to divulge my secret." A sudden shudder went through her and she exhaled, meeting Mitch's concern-filled eyes.

"I understand your hesitation, Nora, believe me. But a good man understands more than you think."

"What man will want a woman like me, Mitch?"

Pain etched Mitch's face at the reminder of the incident which had haunted them both for years. He let out a breath and then looked away from her toward the front door.

"I'm sorry, Mitch. Please, let's not talk about it. It was wrong of me to bring it up."

"I failed you. I couldn't save you."

Nora covered his hand with hers. "You tried, Mitch. He caught us by surprise and was so much larger and stronger than you. Now, stop it. I love you so much for what you did for me that night." A picture formed in her mind of the moonlit night and her brother, bloodied and beaten, lying on the ground. "Whenever I think of that night, it's not only the horror of the attack that gives me nightmares. It's also the sight of you lying there lifeless, in the rain. I was sure he'd killed you."

"Nevertheless, it's time for you to move on. I want you to be happy." Mitch attempted a weak smile. "Bronson Cole is a good man."

"Yes he is," Nora replied and pushed from the table. "But not the man for me, brother."

"Nora..."

"What about Olivia? You went out with her more than once this week?" She lifted an eyebrow at her brother. "Obviously her mother thinks you are courting her."

Mitch shrugged. "I need to get settled first before marrying. Have a house and some sort of life separate from the mercantile. Right now, I don't have anything to call my own. I'm not prepared to offer for anyone's hand."

"Bah!" Nora came up behind him and wrapped her arms around his shoulders pressing her cheek to his hair. "You are not willing to sacrifice your life of leisure. That is what the truth is." She kissed the top of his head. "One of these days, one of the women you lead on will trap you and I'm going to dance a jig at your wedding."

Mitch shook his head and laughed. "Not anytime soon, sister."

Nora sighed. "Poor Mother. It seems she will be repeating today's lecture for many more nights. Dinner will not be complete without questions about our progress into marriage territory." She picked up the dirty plates and carried them through the wide-open doorway to the kitchen.

After scraping the food into a waste bucket, she put the plates into a small tub of hot, soapy water. "I am not looking forward to the harvest picnic at the Cole's ranch next week. Mother will be in full matchmaker mode."

"I, on the other hand, am looking forward to it," Mitch replied from the table. "So many beautiful women gathered in one place." He rubbed his hands together.

"Ah, a wolf into a herd of unsuspecting sheep."

"Not so unsuspecting, sister," he quipped.

"Oh, and the pie-making starts. Mother is already getting the ingredients together." Nora made a face, wrinkling her nose. "I don't think it's fair that you don't have to help Mother make all the pies. The number of pies she decides to bring grows larger every year."

"Loading and unloading them is hard work, as well. Plus, I do help. I bring the sacks of flour from the store, pie tins..." Mitch buckled his gun holster around his waist as he spoke and reached for his hat, his handsome face scrunched in thought. "Come to think of it, I need to check in the shed out behind the store for the crate of pie tins." Mitch stood over six feet tall. He resembled Nora so much that people often asked if they were twins. With chestnut hair, honey brown eyes and full lips, the only difference between them was his strong jawline compared to her softer, pointier chin. "I will see you tomorrow, sister."

His spurs clanked on the hardwood floors as he made his way to the door. Nora turned back to the dishes. "Mitch, you promised to help clean up."

She swung around at the sound of the door closing behind him. "Scoundrel." Left alone, she made quick work of the cleanup. Her mind wandered to Bronson Cole. She'd find him and offer a good excuse to explain her lack of interest in a relationship with him. With a final critical scan of the now clean kitchen, Nora pulled her shawl on over her shoulders.

"Are you leaving so soon?" Her mother looked up from her rocker on the porch when Nora exited the house. "We haven't had our coffee yet."

Nora eyed the sky. It would be dark soon and, although her house was not far, less than a ten minute walk, she preferred not to be out after dark. "Sorry, Mother. I should head home. I have lesson plans to look over." Her mother accepted a hug goodbye and then Nora kissed her father's jaw. She was finally free to head to her cottage next to the town's schoolhouse.

The tiny wooden dwelling welcomed her. The sweet fragrances of lavender and rosemary greeted her as she entered the airy space. It turned out to be a great idea to dry herbs in her small kitchen; they kept the house smelling great.

Nora removed the shawl from her shoulders and folded it before placing it over the back of a chair. It was early yet, too soon for her to go to bed. She went to the kitchen and placed a teakettle on the stove. The silence soothed the troubles of the day. The fatigue of tending to the classroom and helping at the mercantile faded in her quiet, aromatic home.

Although her mother had balked and even attempted to forbid her from moving out of the family's house, she was glad now to have stood her ground. The position of schoolteacher included the small, yet attractive, cottage and Nora seized the opportunity to exercise her need for independence.

As soon as she realized marriage was not in her future, Nora created a new vision for what her life would be. This was part of her new dream. Finding a career and not having to rely on her parents for her entire life were the perfect solutions for a woman who would not marry. Besides, the farther she got from her mother, the easier it was to keep her secret of why she couldn't accept Bronson's proposal. A husband and children, of course she longed for them, and maybe, one day, she'd meet a man willing to overlook her predicament. One day, she'd have the courage to divulge it to the right person. But the thought of sharing what had happened to her made Nora sick to her stomach.

The teakettle whistled and she poured the steaming water into a sturdy mug. She settled into an oversized chair in the front room and drank the tea while reading a book on English history. A shadow crossed the window and she looked across the room following the movement. Her heart skipped when a thump sounded against the door. Clutching the book to her chest, she sat frozen, her eyes glued to the door.

"Nora?" Mitch called from the other side. "Open the door, I brought the pie tins."

Nora jumped to her feet and unlocked the door to a tower of pie tins in Mitch's arms. "Why in the world did you bring them here? We'll only have to take them over to the house in the next couple of days."

Mitch struggled to find a place to set the tins down, so Nora took pity on him and lifted some from the top of the pile to place on her small kitchen table. When her brother attempted to lower the rest, half of them fell to the floor with a clatter of bangs and pings.

"Why did you bring them here?" Nora asked again. "Mitch?" She tapped her foot, not moving to pick up any of the tins. "Answer me."

"I thought I should take care of it now. That's all."

A bark of laughter erupted and Nora shook her head. "You're hiding from someone, aren't you?"

At least he had the decency to look chagrined. "Yeah, Olivia. I sent her a note that I could not call tonight, too busy helping with these." He picked up a pie pan and placed it on the stack on the table. "Walking here, I had to cross in front of her house. I'll take them to the house tomorrow."

"Come sit, I'll make you some tea." Nora pushed him toward the front room. "You have to tell me how you plan to fend off Mother when she asks about it. Because I guarantee you, Olivia's mother will report this."

"Darn it, you're right," Mitch said before slumping against the doorjamb. "I don't need any tea, thank you."

Fists on her hips, Nora leaned forward, her eyes meeting Mitch's. "You're going to the saloon, aren't you? Mitch, I worry about you. I really do."

"And I'll consider it while I drink a whiskey." He tapped the brim of his hat and sauntered through the doorway. "Good night, sister." The door closed firmly behind him.

With a huff, Nora wandered back to the front room. She picked up the book again, but could not bring herself to read. Mitch drank too much. She'd actually been glad to hear that he was distracted from the saloon by visiting with Olivia Dougherty, but now it seemed he was avoiding the poor girl and back to drinking with his friends.

Since the night they'd both rather forget, he'd been different. Although still the caring brother she'd always loved, his nature seemed darker, almost self-destructive at times. If only she could take away the guilt he felt at not being able to stop the man from hurting her.

Chapter Two

From the front porch of their expansive two-story cabin, Elizabeth Cole had the perfect view of the entire area planned for the fall festival activities. "Grayson, place more chairs around those two tables on the end," his mother commanded using a broomstick to point. She looked to his older brother. "Ashley, help your brother."

A chair in each hand, Grayson hurried toward the tables to place them where his mother instructed. With an additional set of chairs, Ashley caught up with him grumbling, "I think my sergeant could have taken lessons from Ma."

"The cavalry could use Ma that's for sure," Grayson replied with a smile. One of the chairs collided with his shin and he grunted. "Seems to me this shindig gets bigger every year."

"Yeah," Ashley replied and rushed back to get another set of chairs.

Grayson followed him only to stop when his twin brother, Bronson, let out a loud yowl and jumped to his feet to hop in a circle with his left hand cradled against his stomach. "Dagnabbit!" Bronson and their father, Hank, were to the left of the house, hammering planks of wood to form what would be a stand for the musicians.

Hank watched Bronson for a moment and then got up from where he was hammering and went to his son. "Let me see, Bronson."

Bronson held out his hand. "I busted my thumb. It'll be all right. I just need to wait a few minutes so I can see straight."

They'd been working on the stage since dawn. Grayson neared and waited for Bronson to look his way. "I can finish up. Why don't you go see about gettin' that thumb wrapped? Looks pretty bad."

Bronson's matching blue eyes met Grayson's for a moment. With dirt streaked across his flushed face, he reminded Grayson of the twelve-year-old version of his now twenty-eight-year-old brother. "Yeah, I suppose I better go and see if Ma will wrap it for me."

"Bronson!" their mother called from the porch. "Get over here and let me look at that thumb."

"How does she do that?" Grayson asked no one in particular. "It's amazing that she can see this far."

"Grayson, stop talking and let your brother come here. Hank, drink some water. It's too hot for you to be out there for this long without drinking."

With a chuckle, his father went to do as she bid and Grayson picked up the hammer.

He'd finished nailing the last of the planks of wood when his father returned from drinking water and whatever other things Ma had him do. "Good job, son. Looks like we're done and ready for the festivities tomorrow."

"I heard several families from Roswell County are coming. You sure we'll have enough seating?" Grayson took a mug of water his father offered and drank deeply. "It's a lot of people."

"They can picnic, plenty of land here for that. Your mother is hoping some young lady catches your or one of your brothers' attention. She's ready for you boys to settle down." He sat next to Grayson on the newly built deck and looked back toward the open land. "Got to start building another house for when Bronson decides to start a family of his own. Your house is still in good condition, waiting for a family, too."

Heaviness pressed at his chest and Grayson pushed it away. It was easier to do now, although it was hard to picture anyone in his kitchen other than Sophia. At Grayson's stoic expression, his father nudged his shoulder. "It's time to move on, Gray. It's time to live your life. Bronson, too. I'm not sure why that boy hasn't married yet."

"Yeah, he's probably got his heart set on someone in particular knowing him."

They did not bring up Ashley. No woman in the neighboring towns would be interested in the loner. There were too many rumors circulating about the mostly silent man, which made people nervous.

Since he'd returned after being discharged from the cavalry for undisclosed reasons, speculation about what actually happened had spread throughout Alder Gulch. There was talk he'd lost his mind in battle and killed a fellow soldier. Gossip abounded about Ashley being unstable. That had held since Ashley refused to talk to anyone outside the family.

Yes, he'd returned changed and although he refused to speak of what happened to him, around the family, he was relatively the same. The biggest changes were a scar across his jawline and his nightmares, which came often. In his terror, his screams woke the entire family until one day he moved to the bunkhouse, where he now lived.

Hank let out a breath and pointed toward the porch where Elizabeth was pulling Bronson into a chair and wrapping a cloth around his neck and shoulders. "Hair cuttin' time."

"I don't need a haircut." Grayson raked his fingers through long, wavy hair and got to his feet. "I'll be in the barn, Pa. Tell Ma I don't want a haircut."

"Right."

Half an hour later, Grayson sat in the chair on the

porch. "Ow, Ma, that hurts! You don't have to pull the comb so hard though my hair." Feeling like a child, he grimaced in silence when she yanked the offensive item through again.

"If you quit fidgeting, it won't hurt as much. It's just so darn tangled. Honestly, Gray, your hair is down to here." She pushed a finger into the center of his shoulder blades. "How did we ever let it get so long?"

She continued combing through it, not one snip of her scissors sounded. "It's so beautiful, the color of chestnuts."

He looked over his shoulder and smiled up at her. "You say that every time and then don't cut but a bit." He drew his brows together. "Why do you cut Bronson's hair short and not mine?"

"For a long time, because it was easier to tell you two apart from a distance." She chuckled. "Your father used to get so mad at me. He said I was trying to make you a girl since we didn't have one. He was always threatening to take you to the barber shop in town." She ran her fingers through his hair and Grayson smiled at her hesitation to cut his too-long mane. "Now I suppose it's because I just got used to you always having longer hair."

"I'm all right with it being long, Ma. I don't mind."

Her wide smile lightened his heart. "I'm glad to hear it, son. I'll trim it just a little then."

That evening, Ashley strummed the guitar on the front porch while Grayson and Bronson took turns throwing a lasso around a pole they'd planted in the ground. Bronson's newly sheared hair fell across his brow when he leaned forward to pull his rope from around the beam. "I hear there are some pretty girls over in Roswell County." He gave Grayson an expectant look. "Maybe you and ol' Ashley will get motivated and find a wife."

Ashley stopped strumming and glowered at Bronson's back. "What?"

"What about you?" Grayson replied, ignoring Ashley. "You have someone in mind?"

Bronson slid his eyes to the left, a sure sign he was about to lie. "Nope, keeping my options open."

"Well, I, for one, am not planning on getting tied down any time soon. Tried it once. Lookin' forward to the pretty women comin' though."

"You are one step ahead of us then," Bronson replied and tossed the rope without even looking at the stump. He missed.

"I think you got someone in mind," Grayson told his twin and watched for a reaction.

"I don't," Bronson replied after sliding his eyes to the side. "I'm not interested in marrying any time soon either, so Ma's going to be mad at us."

Grayson wrapped the rope around his elbow. "I'm going inside. We've got an early day tomorrow."

"What about you, Ashley?" Bronson was the only one who dared ask the sullen brother such a question. Ashley pointedly ignored him.

"Ashley, I'm talkin' to you," Bronson repeated and threw the rope at his older brother's boot and then pulled on his leg.

Ashley frowned and yanked his leg back. "Women avoid me like the plague, so you figure it out."

"Maybe if you let your hair grow like Gray, then they'll chase you like they do him."

Scowl in place, Ashley studied Grayson. "Yeah, right. They probably think he's a woman in disguise."

Grayson laughed. "Only 'til they catch me."

"Boys!" their mother called from the kitchen. "Anyone want coffeecake?"

"Yes, ma'am," they replied in unison.

Chapter Three

It was hard to ignore the lush expanse of the open ranchlands framed by a backdrop of the mountains and a clear blue sky. The over-laden wagon rocked in a steady rhythm as horses traversed the smooth trail. The day was bright. It was still early morning, yet it felt late to Nora. Up since dawn to bake the last of the pies, exhaustion settled into her shoulders. Even the short nap on the ride from town out to the edge of the Coles' ranch did little to help.

"Oh, goodness, look at all the people." Nora's mother bounced in the backbench seat with excitement. "I can't wait to hear the new fiddler you've been talking so much about," she told her husband who smiled in return at her enthusiasm.

Nora glanced to Mitch. He sat on the bench next to her, guiding the horses. "It's a perfect day for the festival, sunny, but not too warm." She looked across the expanse of the Coles' ranch and inhaled the fresh air. Several chestnut horses grazed in the corrals, their tails swishing back and forth. Farther away, she spotted a large herd of brown spotted cows, some grazing, some laying in the shade, seeming to enjoy the fresh morning.

People milled about the picnic area and she admired the huge farmhouse; the two-story, proud structure was remarkable. A long front porch with rounded archways held several rocking chairs. Most of the rockers had people sitting in them. The log home's enormous front door was open, giving the impression everyone was welcome to enter.

Nora had only been inside the Coles' home once, when Elizabeth Cole, the matron, invited the townswomen for an afternoon tea. Nora had been invited several times after, but could never attend since she taught class every day until late afternoon.

A tall, muscular man appeared at the doorway and leaned against the jamb. Hat in hand, he looked at ease. His head turned from side to side as he scanned the area, overlooking his family's land. Grayson Cole.

Nora squinted to get a better look at him. His hair was shorter than the last time she'd spotted him in town, but still longer than most men's. Touching his shoulders, the burnished waves blew away from his face. From this distance, she could not make out his eyes, but she knew them to be bright blue. It was an eye color she'd never seen until meeting the Cole twins. Although Grayson and Bronson were almost identical, it was Grayson who stole her breath every time she saw him. Just a bit broader at the shoulders than his twin, he was also the more easy-going of the two. Unlike his brothers, Grayson was a ladies man. Every time she'd seen him in town, a different woman hung on his arm. Although known for his rakish ways, he never suffered for companionship. One woman after another hoped to be the one to tame the handsome male.

Her brother brought the wagon close to where a large tent was erected. Under the tent, long picnic tables were set, some already brimming with offerings. Nora continued to watch Grayson, soaking in the rare moment of him standing still and, rarer yet, alone.

As if sensing her regard, his sharp gaze met hers and Nora felt her cheeks heat. He lifted his hand in greeting and Mitch waved in return.

"Hello, Bronson." Her mother's breathless voice tore Nora's attention from Grayson to notice that Bronson approached the wagon. He looked up at Nora and offered his hand to assist her down.

The warmth in Bronson's brilliant blue eyes was hard to ignore. Nora forced a soft smile and accepted his help. "Nice to see you, Nora." Bronson's deep voice and heated regard made her flush. "You look very nice today."

"Thank you," she murmured turning to grab her small satchel. When she looked again, Bronson had gone to the back of the wagon to help unload the pies.

Nora waited until they headed toward the tent with the first large tray before she went to the back of the wagon to get a couple pies to carry. When she turned and took a step, she ran into Grayson's firm chest, almost dropping a pie. "Oh! I apologize, Grayson. I didn't see you."

Deep blue eyes regarded her. He didn't reply and Nora lifted her eyebrows. "It's customary to accept an apology."

"It is, isn't it?" Grayson replied, a corner of his lips lifted in mocking. "It's also customary to look where you're going before walking, to make sure you are not about to trample someone."

"What?" Nora could only gawk at the rude man. "I did not come close to trampling you."

He shrugged and leaned over the back of the wagon. His wide back strained when he lifted an entire tray of pies. Nora gritted her teeth together in frustration at not being able to stop her eyes from admiring him.

"Blasted man."

"Who are you talking about, dear?" Her mother touched Nora's elbow, her sharp gaze taking in Grayson. "Ah yes, he can be bothersome. It's a wonder they were able to get him married off the one time."

At the mention of Grayson's disastrous marriage, Nora's eyes flew back to him. Hopefully, he didn't hear her mother. "Mother, keep your voice down."

"I ensured no one heard me," her mother whispered

and pulled her forward. "Let me take one of these. The men can get the rest." Carolyn took one of the pies from Nora and prompted her daughter to walk with her.

"Whatever happened to his wife?" Nora asked following her mother away from the food tent a few minutes later.

"Oh goodness, the poor thing." Her mother looked over her shoulder to make sure no one was close. "It was horrible. It seems her horse was spooked and she fell off, but her foot got caught in the stirrup. The horse dragged her to death. Only two weeks after getting married." Carolyn shook her head. "That boy was heartbroken. He hasn't been the same since."

Nora stopped walking. Too stunned, she held her hand over her mouth. She could only imagine the horror the poor woman went through. Her heart broke for Grayson at losing his young wife so soon after marrying.

"Are you all right?" Bronson came up behind her and she inhaled sharply.

"Yes, I'm fine, thank you. Just a bit tired from the ride out here. Mother and I were up late baking." She slipped her hand through his proffered arm. "Your mother has outdone herself, everything looks perfect."

The handsome man chuckled. "Yes, she has kept us busy for the last two weeks in preparation." His eyes met hers and she fought not to look away at seeing the matching shade of blue to Grayson's. "Save me a dance later, please." His quiet request made her soften and she could only nod.

"Well, I better go see about the newcomers," Bronson told her. He turned to head toward two wagonloads of people who had just arrived.

Nora's father found a free area under a small tree and the family spread a blanket and settled for the day. Her mother, always prepared, brought two thick pillows and her sewing basket. Nora leaned on one of the pillows, her elbow sinking into it and soaked in the atmosphere. It was definitely a well-attended event.

She caught sight of Hank and Elizabeth Cole walking from table to table, welcoming guests. Hank was tall and broad shouldered like his sons. With grey intermingling through his light brown hair, Hank Cole remained an attractive man. His wife murmured something to him and his lips curved in response, his warm gaze taking her in. Elizabeth Cole was of medium build with golden brown hair that she wore in a long braid down her back. Together they made a stunning couple.

The Coles approached her family and her father jumped to his feet, shaking Hank's hand. "Thank you for hosting such a fine event. I do believe the entire town is here." His bright eyes settled on Nora. "Nora is glad to get an opportunity to see your son."

Mortified at her father's words, Nora's eyes flew wide open and she looked to Elizabeth Cole, who smiled at her with a questioning look. The woman pulled her hand from her husband's and came to where Nora and her mother now stood. "It's nice to see you, Carolyn, Nora." She embraced each of them, but kept her hand on Nora's forearm and leaned in to whisper into her ear. "Don't worry, darling. I'm sure your father didn't mean to embarrass you. But whichever of my sons you choose, I'd be glad about it."

"Thank you, Missus Cole," Nora sputtered, not sure what to think of the statement.

After a few minutes of conversation, the Coles moved on to greet another family.

"Where's Mitch?" Carolyn motioned for Nora to sit next to her. "He seems to have disappeared."

Nora searched across the area, but did not spot him. "I'm sure he's about."

An hour later, Mitch had still not appeared. Nora figured he was off stealing a moment with a lady. "Nora, be a dear and go fetch Mitch. I need him to see about taking the wagon to the barn and loosening the horses to graze," her mother prompted. Nora agreed to go in hunt of him.

The musicians began playing a lively jig and she ducked toward the barn before Bronson could make his way over to claim his dance. As much as she liked Bronson, there was no way she could allow a courtship with him. It wouldn't be fair to him that when seeing the similar face, she'd constantly think of Grayson. They looked too much alike; Nora would not hurt Bronson that way. Although if she were to be honest with herself, he was a better fit for her, yet for some odd reason, she found it impossible to think of him as a husband.

The dimness of the barn was a welcome relief from the bright sun and the noise of the festivities.

Nora peeked into several stables. Most of them were empty, the horses having been put out to enjoy the spring day. "Mitch?" she called out, hoping he wasn't in the hayloft with a woman. When no response came, she considered continuing out to the other side to check behind the dwelling, but the thought of walking up on a couple who had stolen away made her desist. Instead, she eyed the ladder to the hayloft. Nora stole a glance over her shoulder; there was no one around but her. Before she knew it, her satchel slipped onto her arm, she climbed the ladder to the hayloft.

Up in the loft, the air remained fresh, which told her that the Coles took proper care to ensure fresh hay was kept in the barn for the animals. With caution, she sat on the soft bundle of hay and let out a sigh. Beams of sunlight streaked in from a small window across the loft and she considered what a good place this would be for a short nap. Surely her mother would think she was walking about talking to her students' parents and wouldn't worry for at least an hour. Plenty of time for her to doze and get a few minutes of much needed rest. A yawn confirmed her plan and Nora pulled a shawl from her satchel to spread over the hay.

Her eyes closed as soon as she lay back onto the comfortable hay. With a deep breath, she smiled at the wonderful turn of events. A soft breeze caressed her face and she sighed. Of all places to find peace, she never expected to find it here, so near to Grayson Cole.

Footsteps sounded, not loud, just enough to jerk Nora awake. Then the steps stopped and whoever it was began to climb the ladder. Nora scrambled backward, but there was no place to hide, she wasn't about to duck behind the hay. Goodness, was a couple coming to steal some time together? Maybe she'd make a noise and they'd realize someone was already up in the loft.

Her eyes widened when Grayson Cole's face appeared over the ledge of the loft. She blinked to compose her face and waited for him to notice she was there. He looked over his shoulder and she wondered who the woman would be climbing up after him.

When he turned to face her, his mouth fell open and his eyebrows disappeared under the hair that fell across his forehead. "What are you doing here?" His words came out clipped. Obviously she was about to spoil his plans.

"I came searching for Mitch," she replied watching his leg swing over the edge. "You can't mean to come up while I'm here." Nora put her hand out to stop him. "Go away, Grayson."

Instead of leaving, he climbed up and lowered himself to the hay. He gifted her with a lazy look. "Nope, not leaving. Your brother is obviously not here, so who are you really meeting up with?"

"What? I am not meeting anyone," Nora hissed, resisting the urge to slap the smirk off his face. "After finding Mitch was not here, I decided to rest a bit."

The beautiful, blue eyes slid from her face down to where her shawl was spread on the hay. "Looks like a love nest to me."

"Well, if it were, then *you* are definitely not welcome to be here," she said, emphasizing the word "you".

Instead of making to leave, he picked up a hay straw and placed it between his teeth. He studied her until she began to fidget. "It so happens, I came here to get a few minutes of quiet myself. So Miss Banks, would *you* please leave. We wouldn't want someone to happen upon the prim and proper little schoolteacher and the town rake up here together, now would we?"

"You are no gentleman, Grayson Cole. You should leave immediately so that such a thing doesn't happen."

"You said it. I'm no gentleman." He took the straw out of his mouth and tossed it away, only to pick up another one. "Go on now, get yourself down the ladder. Be careful." He motioned toward the ladder.

"Grayson, if you don't leave now, I am going to push you off." Nora's heart quickened and she let out an annoyed breath at the arrogant man's lack of manners. "Get on now." She pushed at his shoulder with both hands and, of course, he barely budged. "Go!"

"Nope."

"Grayson, go away!" In her anger she forgot to keep her voice down.

"Be careful, before we both fall." He put a hand down to ensure she could not move him. "Here, I'll help you get down." Grayson took both her upper arms in his hands and attempted to lift her from sitting. "Darn it," he cursed when his knee slipped.

The next thing Nora knew, she was flat on her back and Grayson was on top of her. Wind knocked from her, she could only stare at the handsome face. Not even in her dreams had she ever dared think of him being this close. Grayson lifted up, straightening his arms, his eyes darkening when they met hers. "Well, Miss Banks. I would apologize, but this is your fault for not leaving. Now, we are certainly in a compromising position."

Her head demanded she push him away and scream, but her mouth and arms partnered against her. He felt so heavy but, at the same time, the proximity of his body to hers made her want to wrap her arms around him. When her gaze lowered to his mouth, the rake had the nerve to chuckle. "Not today, darlin'."

"Of all the arrogant, most dreadful beings!" Nora pushed at him. "Get off me."

"What's going on up there?"

Oh no, Mitch.

Grayson rolled off and sat next to her, while Nora jerked upright.

"Nothing," both she and Grayson replied at the same time. Nora almost giggled at the frown Grayson directed at her.

"Like hell," Mitch replied, climbing up the ladder. "Grayson, what the hell are you doing up there with my sister?" He reached the top of the ladder and glowered at them. "Get down from here, Nora," he instructed and grabbed Grayson's boot. "You, too, Grayson. Come down and face me."

"Not until you listen to me, Mitch. This is a misunderstanding." Grayson yanked his leg back. "I climbed up here not knowing she was here."

"And somehow ended up on top of her?" Mitch's eyes narrowed. "I know what I saw."

"He slipped," Nora said, but when a giggle escaped, the words fell hollow. "Mitch, climb down and we'll follow."

Mitch growled and yanked at Grayson's foot again. "You'll make this right, Grayson." He pulled at the boot with force and Grayson's foot slipped out of it. Mitch's eyes widened with realization right before both he and the boot disappeared from sight.

Nora screamed and Grayson scrambled to look down to where Mitch landed. All was quiet for about two seconds and she decided to crawl beside Grayson to look over the edge.

"Oh God, Mitch!" Nora shrieked at seeking her brother on his back, his mouth opening and closing, the air knocked out of his lungs.

Twin shadows fell over Mitch and her blood ran cold. Both Hank Cole and her father rushed to where Mitch lay and both looked up in unison at her and Grayson.

Her father found his voice first. "What in the hell is going on here?"

Mitch sat up and shook his head. Of course, his voice returned right before Nora could tell her father that it was all an unfortunate misunderstanding. "I interrupted Grayson attempting to have his way with Nora," Mitch announced. Her father's narrowed eyes lifted up to the loft and then turned to Grayson's father. "Hank, your boy is going do right by my daughter. He has disrespected my family and I won't stand for it." Without looking back at her, he spoke to Nora next. "Nora, get yourself down here. Of all the things for a woman your age to do."

It was incredible that her father actually thought she'd sneak away with a man in the middle of a town picnic. Not sure what to do, she looked to Grayson who gave her a bored shrug. "I'll go down first and help you." He began to climb down, his mocking blue gaze meeting hers as he descended. "Come now, Nora."

She climbed down without looking below, too preoccupied with what she'd say to her father. When she reached the bottom, Mitch shoved Grayson out of the way. "Keep your hands off my sister."

"For goodness sakes," Nora's voice was loud with anger. "It's all a huge misunderstanding. Nothing happened between us. We can barely cross two words without arguing." She looked past her father to where Grayson stood next to Hank, who more than anything seemed to be amused. "Tell them, Grayson. Don't just stand there."

Everyone turned to look at the cowboy who frowned as if in thought. "I went up to the loft to relax. Found Nora there."

That was all he planned to say? "And?" Nora prompted.

"Why were you on top of my sister when I came in?" Mitch asked

Grayson shrugged. "I slipped when she was trying to

push me off the loft." He went to Mitch and snatched his boot. "That's the truth. I didn't..."

"You'll marry my daughter," her father interrupted and Nora gasped.

"What?" both she and Grayson exclaimed in unison.

"How could you?" A red-faced blond, Amy Foster, picked the worst time to walk in and Nora finally found out the woman Grayson really planned to meet. The girl didn't seemed to care about anyone else standing in the barn, because she stomped over to a startled Grayson and slapped him across the face. "I knew it. When your brother said you went to the barn, you were meeting someone else. I never thought it was her you were rolling in the hay with." She directed a sharp look towards Nora.

"I did not roll in the hay with him," Nora snapped.

"Enough." Hank Cole's deep voice cut through and everyone looked to the man who now put his hand on Amy's shoulder, possibly in an effort to keep her from hitting Grayson again. "Amy, you've misunderstood. Would you please excuse us? Grayson just told me he planned to ask you to dance shortly."

Amy softened and her lips curved up at the elder Cole. "Oh, that would be lovely."

Once she left, Hank shook his head. "Arthur, if your family will please remain until after the festivities end this evening, then we can all talk in private. I will apprise Elizabeth. Come on, son. We'll have a talk now."

Dread filled her when the Coles left and she swung to her father. "Why did you say he has to marry me? Surely you don't believe anything happened, Father."

Arthur Banks' shrewd eyes met hers evenly. "It's only proper. After the compromising position your brother found you in."

"Grayson Cole told the truth. I was attempting to shove him off the loft and he slipped."

"Be that as it may, it's a blessing in disguise." Her father walked away as if the matter were settled.

She gawked at him and turned to Mitch. "Do something."

"What can I possibly do? Father has that look in his eye. He's made up his mind of how it will be handled. You just stumbled upon a way for him to make Mother happy."

Realization dawned and her knees wobbled. Her parents would push this. They'd see it as a way to get their spinster daughter married and finally have grandchildren.

"Oh for goodness sakes," Nora said and glared at her brother. "Look what you did."

Chapter Four

"What are you planning to say to the Banks' later, Pa?" A tingle of fear trickled up Grayson's spine at his father's stern expression. They left the barn and headed straight for where his mother stood with Bronson. Mother and son overlooked the carving of the meat by several of the ranch hands.

"We'll speak of it in a minute. Let me get your mother. For now, go help Ashley out back."

Banished, Grayson did not argue. It was best to keep from angering his father. Although he knew the final decision would be his regardless of what the parents decided, he worried about his hand being forced by Arthur Banks.

His mother's eyes flashed from his father's face to him.

"Hold up, Grayson," Hank said while watching his wife.

Elizabeth's brows knit together. Perceptive as always, she rushed to meet them before they got close enough to be overheard. "What happened, Hank?" She reached for Hank's hand and was immediately pulled into his side.

"It's nothing too serious. Grayson, here, got caught with the Banks girl up in the hayloft."

Elizabeth Cole burst into laughter, which continued until she had to wipe tears from her eyes. Her eyes twinkled when meeting Grayson's. "You're both a bit too old for that, aren't you?" She began to chuckle again.

"Ma, I didn't mean to be up there with her. I went to get away from Amy Foster who's been constantly finding a way to be around me. Unfortunately, Nora was there and then her brother and father came upon us." He left off the part of him crushing Nora for fear his mother would start laughing again.

She patted his arm. "Don't worry, sweetheart. I'm sure it'll all be worked out. Goodness, Grayson, it's the last thing I expected today. You in a hayloft with Nora Banks."

His father kissed Elizabeth's forehead and got her attention. "Her father is demanding Grayson marry the girl due to the compromising situation in which her brother claims to have found them."

"Oh goodness," his mother replied, her eyes sliding towards where the Banks' sat. "Arthur Banks is not usually so demanding, although this is his only daughter."

"I'm not marrying her, Ma," Grayson interjected. "Nothing happened. Her parents are just trying to get her married off since she's a spins..."

"Grayson Cole, don't you dare call that poor girl a name. She's probably your age, if not a year younger," his mother admonished. "Why women are looked down upon if they're not married by twenty is beyond me."

"Calm down, dear." his father soothed her. "Let's decide what we're going to do about this before we have to talk with the Banks'." His father spoke while rubbing her arm.

Elizabeth Cole met Grayson's eyes and she softened. "It would not be a bad match. Nora is a beautiful girl. And if her father demands for her honor's sake, you cannot deny it, Grayson. It would be horrible for Nora if word got out that she was taking a tumble with you up in the hay loft."

A sick feeling descended into his belly and Grayson could only gape at his mother.

"Now, now," she soothed. "What if you agree to court

the girl, spend time with her and see if you are a match? Perhaps they'll agree to that. And who knows, maybe you'll change your mind."

Grayson took the hat off his head and wiped his brow. "I sure hope so, Ma. 'Cause I'm not getting married by force." He looked across the field and saw that the Banks' were making their way toward the food tent. Carolyn Banks was wringing her hands, her husband speaking to her with hurried hand gestures. Nora, however, remained behind, her head bent over a book in her lap. Oblivious to her surroundings, lost in her reading, she seemed without a care. His heart lightened. Perhaps she'd convinced her parents against the needless talk of marriage.

As if sensing his regard, she lifted her head and her eyes met his. The distress displayed on her face made his heart pitch and his gut sink again. They held gazes and Grayson felt an unexpected compulsion to go over to where she was and comfort her. When his father's hand touched his shoulder, he broke eye contact.

His father blew out a breath. "Let's see what happens, Gray. It'll all get worked out, you'll see."

The day passed without incident. Nora finally gave in and danced with Bronson while maintaining an ongoing conversation with him about the ranch and the weather. Finally, she and her family made their way into the Coles' home.

Her face felt too hot. Nora could only imagine how red it was. At her age, the town's schoolteacher for God's sakes, and here she was, waiting in the Coles' front room to be paraded before the Coles. What an embarrassment. Bronson walked in and gave her a questioning look to which Nora responded with what she was sure was a weak smile.

The festivities had ended over an hour earlier. The last of the families finally departed late in the day or set up camp nearby which allowed for them to finally have privacy. Grayson came in to view as he passed the doorway with his older brother, Ashley. They carried a table toward the kitchen. Grayson had been busy fetching furniture or tearing down temporary tents since she'd come inside. Nora figured they usually left those things for the next day, but he was keeping busy to avoid being in the same room with her.

"Would you like something to drink?" Bronson asked, his eyes sliding toward their parents who'd yet to get past the pleasantries.

"No, thank you. I've had more than my fill today." Nora looked out the window to note the sunlight was almost completely gone.

"Are you staying here tonight?" He neared and sat next to her. "Is there something wrong?"

Nora swallowed, not sure how to answer his question. Bronson had made it abundantly clear he was interested in her. He did not deserve to be hurt. "You could say that. It was a misunderstanding..."

"Bronson dear, would you please fetch Grayson and tell him to come in here?" Elizabeth interrupted. "And remain out of this room with Ashley. This matter has to be settled with Grayson only." Her kind eyes went to Nora for a moment then back to her son.

Bronson's blue gaze moved around the room, his brows scrunched as he tried to figure out what had brought the meeting between the families. He looked to Mitch, who remained sprawled in a chair opposite Nora. Mitch shrugged at him.

"Go with him, Mitch," her mother interjected. Mitch, more than eager to avoid the discussion, jumped to his feet and walked out.

The Coles' maid came in with a tray and began to pour coffee into blue-speckled, porcelain mugs.

Carolyn sat next to Nora and took her hand. "Now, now, honey, just relax." Nora shot her mother an annoyed look, but managed to keep from snatching her hand away. Just like her mother to play this up and make the Coles think she was on the brink of a breakdown.

"I'm fine, Mother," she replied with an even voice. Nora looked toward Hank and Elizabeth Cole. "I'm sorry for all this, but like both Grayson and I already stated, it's all a huge misunderstanding."

"That's true," Grayson agreed as he stood at the doorway, his large frame filling it completely. With hands to his sides and shoulder on the jamb, he gave the impression of complete unconcern.

"Not from where Mitch stood," replied her father. Arthur stood and glared at Grayson. "You were practically er...well on top of her."

Carolyn gasped and Nora looked up to the ceiling wishing it would fall on top of her. Unfortunately, her father continued in his campaign to get her married off. "The rumors are already spreading. Little Amy Foster told everyone who'd listen about the situation in the barn."

"Oh goodness," Elizabeth Cole exclaimed and frowned at her husband who covered her hand with his much larger one.

"Of course, we want to protect Nora's reputation being that she's Alder Gulch's schoolmarm. So how about it, son?" Elizabeth Cole looked to Grayson whose eyes widened and he swallowed visibly.

"I—I would like to offer to...seek a courtship with Miss Nora," he straightened, his posture straight and looked at her father. "Mister Banks, nothing happened, I assure you. I would never disrespect your daughter in that manner."

"Of course nothing happened," her father exclaimed lifting to his toes as if attempting to match Grayson's height. "Because Mitch walked in on you." He glared over his shoulder at Nora with a perfected "Don't say a thing" look.

Grayson did not back down. "Like I said, Mister Banks, I would never steal away with her. She's above reproach." His jaw clenched. "I'm not offering anything more."

I'm not his type is more like it. Nora closed her eyes to

avoid, for a few seconds, witnessing the circus the situation had become. When Hank Cole placed his cup down and stood, she braced herself for what was to come next.

The large male stepped between her father and Grayson. He met his son's eyes. "Sit down, Grayson. Getting angry is not helping things."

After Grayson sat down in the chair Mitch had vacated, Hank Cole turned to her father. "Now, Arthur, I believe my boy's offer to court your daughter is enough to waylay any rumors."

"Until he moves on," her mother exclaimed with narrowed eyes directed at Grayson. "He's the town rake, everyone knows that."

"Mother, Mitch isn't much better," Nora told her, not sure why she needed to defend Grayson, who looked at her with lifted eyebrows. "This is ridiculous." No longer able to remain silent, she got to her feet. "Grayson and I are not teenagers. I assure everyone that we can work this out without all this—this." She waved her hands in the air, not sure what to call the proceedings.

She looked to Grayson for help, but he remained seated, his mouth firmly shut. *Annoying.* "I accept Grayson's offer to court me. We will court until the rumors die down, which they will. As far as my reputation being ruined after he moves on, well, what's the difference? I'm the town spinster now. And I wouldn't marry the likes of Grayson Cole anyway."

"What?" Finally, he decided to speak just when she wanted him not to. "What do you mean by 'the likes of me'?" He frowned up at her.

"Unfaithful," Nora replied, lowering back to the couch while keeping her gaze on him.

"Nora, enough." Carolyn squeezed Nora's forearm. Her fingers sinking into the flesh until Nora winced. "We won't accept less than a marriage proposal." She eyed Elizabeth Cole. "Surely you see the gravity of this situation. If we leave it up to the two of them, they'll only make things worse." She dabbed at the corner of her eye with a handkerchief that seemed to have appeared out of thin air. "I can't bear any more insults from your son toward my daughter. Not wanting to make amends for what he did up in that hayloft." She sniffed into the handkerchief hiding her face behind it.

"Mother," Nora hissed, "what are you doing?"

"Fine! Enough of this nonsense." Hank Cole finally raised his voice and everyone turned to him. "Grayson, you'll marry Nora. You need to settle down anyway."

This time, it was Nora who gasped. She looked to Grayson who looked straight ahead, his face stoic. Grayson nodded. "Yes, sir."

Carolyn grabbed Nora's arm and pulled her toward the front door. "Fine. You will call on her this Sunday." Too numb to resist and stunned silent, Nora followed her mother out. Her father remained behind. She heard him say something, but the words did not penetrate the fog enveloping her.

"Come along, Nora. How distressing! It is horrible how that cad tried to get out of doing the right thing."

"Nora?" Elizabeth Cole walked out to the porch and stopped them. "Are you all right, dear?"

Nora fought the overwhelming desire to cry. "I'm sorry for walking out."

"It's so distressing," her mother told Grayson's mother, her voice quivering. "I just had to come out here and get some fresh air."

"Of course." Elizabeth guided her mother to a chair on the porch while Nora looked on dumbfounded. How did this all become about her mother?

The men exited, first her father, then Hank Cole and, finally, Grayson, who looked more tired than angry. He went to Nora and she stiffened. She lifted her gaze to him. "Good night, Grayson."

He nodded. "Would you care to go for a ride after church on Sunday?"

Their parents stopped the pretense and looked to them. Weary, she nodded to him. "Yes, of course."

After she and her mother were seated in the carriage, Mitch came out and climbed onto the bench next to Nora. He brought the horses to a quick trot and immediately the ambiance changed.

"Oh, Nora, your wedding should be out here on Cole lands. I can see it now. It will be the most talked about wedding for years." Her mother seemed to have rebounded from being upset with frightening speed and beamed at her father. "Arthur, we should order plenty of blue fabric. That shade Nora favors. What do you call it, Nora? Peacock blue or something?"

Nora gawked at her mother. Mitch chuckled and she jabbed her elbow into his ribs.

Oblivious to Nora's silence, her mother continued. "Oh, and of course we'll need to look in the catalog for a simple, but pretty, dress for you. White, of course." The prattling continued until they reached town an hour later.

Her head pounded when they finally reached her parent's home. Too exhausted to walk to her house, she climbed the stairs to her old bedroom intent on collapsing into the bed and forgetting everything that had transpired.

After a quick wash with tepid water from the pitcher in her room, she slipped on her nightgown and brushed the tangles from her hair. The house was silent and her tension began to ebb away. Surely Grayson would not be forced into a marriage with her. When he called on Sunday, she'd make the best of it. Together, they'd find a way out of the situation.

She studied her oval face reflecting in the mirror. There were circles under her honey brown eyes, a soft purpling of weariness. Her long lashes framed her half-closed eyes.

Grayson did not find her attractive.

He'd never given any indication of it. If anything, he was more indifferent than interested whenever they'd crossed paths. With a deep sigh, she stopped the musings and brushed the last of the tangles out of her long waves and then braided her hair with quick, efficient fingers. Tomorrow, she'd think clearer and come up with a way to release Grayson of any commitment.

Chapter Five

Grayson remained outside the chapel until the service started before he made his way inside and sat at the back. His parents and Bronson were in their usual spots, fourth bench back from the front. He scanned the large space for Nora but didn't spot her. Truth be told, he never noticed where she and her family sat.

No, he usually gave Nora Banks a wide berth, and if ever they did cross paths, he'd made an excuse to get away, cross the street, anything to not come face-to-face with the beauty. Her large, light brown eyes took away his ability to think clearly. When she spoke, which usually was quick and efficient, his eyes were drawn to her lush, pink lips. Neither small nor overly large, her shapely mouth often took his mind to a place it shouldn't go. When she'd been angered in the loft, her pretty face flushed and as she lay under him, he wanted nothing more than to sink down onto her and kiss the woman until neither could breathe.

A hymn began, bringing his attention back to the present. Once again, he took in the room and, this time, he saw her. In an olive, flowered dress and matching green shawl, she had her head bent, her eyes on the hymnal in her lap. Her lips moved with the song and Grayson watched her until the song ended.

In a few minutes, he'd be forced to spend time alone with her and he wasn't prepared for it. Not that he despised her company so much as he detested his reactions to her. Not since Sophia had a woman gotten his attention like Nora Banks did and for that reason alone, he'd fight with all he had to keep from marrying her. A sharp pain struck him in the chest, taking his breath in a not so subtle reminder of the price of loving someone only to lose them. Nora Banks was not meant for him. She'd one day be someone's wife. She was too beautiful not to be.

Just not his.

The service ended too soon and Grayson got up to leave the chapel before the pastor made his way to the back. He moved to the side of the building and waited for Nora to come out.

Finally, almost half an hour later, she exited. Her burnished hair, pulled into a loose braid down her back that allowed for tendrils to flow in the wind across her face, shimmered in the sunlight. She placed a hand over her eyes and looked around until spotting him. When she did, he could not read the expression on her face. When her eyes raked over him, she tensed. The movement was so quick it may have only been in his imagination. With sure steps, she came toward him, shoulders back and head held high. Grayson's lips curved at knowing she felt the stares of the people still gathered at the church watching them with ill-concealed interest. So it was true. Rumors did circulate about their supposed hayloft tryst.

"Hello, Grayson." Her voice was even although he heard a soft quiver. *Of anger?*

"Miss Banks," he replied and put his arm out to her. "Shall we perform for the crowd?"

With an indignant huff, she slid her gaze towards the chapel without turning her head. "One would think they would have better things to do on a Sunday morning. Especially after the sermon on minding our tongues."

"They're pretty quiet," he quipped back with a chuckle.

"It's not funny, for goodness sakes. Now it will be harder to make them believe it didn't happen. We should not have met here." She walked faster toward the buggy he'd brought from the ranch. "Where are we going, anyway? I hope it's away from town."

"Ma got cook to make us a picnic." Grayson helped her up into the buggy and circled to climb up on the other side. He snuck a glance toward the chapel and, although a few of the people had dispersed, several groups still remained to watch them. One lady even waved at him. The town's latest fodder for gossip, nothing new for him, but Nora wasn't used to it. Judging by the paleness of her face and stiffness of her posture, he figured she would burst into tears.

"Are you all right?" Grayson smiled at her. "Would you prefer to walk for a bit?"

"No. I'm fine," she replied sounding anything but.

They rode in silence until they arrived at a spot near a shallow stream where he'd brought many a lady. Grayson knew the place well and guided the horse between trees so that it could feed and be near enough to the stream to drink water. After climbing down, he went to assist Nora. Hand extended up, it was a few beats before she took it, her eyes on his face. The softness of her hand in his rougher one made him almost retract the offer of assistance. Everything about the woman affected him too much.

Once she descended, she stood by the buggy looking at the view until Grayson grabbed a blanket and handed it to her. He then took the basket by the handles and guided her towards a grassy spot. "This is a nice, peaceful place. I come here often."

They walked a few yards and Nora helped him spread the blanket. Grayson watched her sink down onto it and pull off her hat. Suddenly, he found himself nervous, at a loss for words. He toed the edge of the blanket and looked to the water. "I'm gonna go rinse my hands. Be right back."

Nora shrugged in response and began to dig in her bag. From the water's edge, he watched to see what she did.

Reading? She'd pulled a book out of her bag and was reading. Is this what she planned to do? Did she find his company so distasteful that she'd rather read than have a conversation? Grayson huffed and went back to the blanket and threw himself down on it. On his back, he folded his arms under his head and stared at the sky. "An hour should be long enough to make it seem as if we enjoy each other's company. Wake me will you?" He closed his eyes.

"Fine with me," Nora replied in a bored tone.

Under his lashes, he saw her study him. He fully opened his eyes and looked at her and cocked an eyebrow. "Unless you'd rather do something else?"

Her eyes narrowed. "Like what?"

With slow precision he lowered his gaze to her lips. "What do you think?"

Nora's eyes widened only a bit before she schooled a neutral expression. "I think you're an arrogant libertine."

"From a prudish schoolmarm, I take that as a compliment."

"You know nothing about me."

"I know you keep yourself at arm's length from everyone around you, as if you're too good to be around common folk."

A gasp escaped followed by an unladylike snort. "If because I don't rut around with every person of the opposite sex like you do, in your opinion, I'm an elitist. Well, that's fine with me."

"Women come after me, not the other way around, Miss Banks," Grayson replied and closed his eyes again. "I can't help that your kind finds me an irresistible challenge."

"Is that what you think? Honestly, your arrogance has no bounds."

"I'm being honest."

"This is all a bad idea. We should return before I say something I shouldn't."

This time, he sat up and gawked at her. "I hate to think

41

what that would be. Let's see, you've called me arrogant, a rake and accused me of rutting. Maybe given time, you'll get more creative. It would be a refreshing change. If insulting me amuses you, then by all means." He opened his arms, exposing his wide chest to her.

A slow exhale told him she attempted to keep from lashing back. Her beautiful, honey brown eyes flashed with anger. "Hardly. This is not amusing, Mr. Cole, not in the least."

"Look, I find this as distasteful as you do..."

"Distasteful?" She scrambled to her feet and glared down at him with her hands on her hips. "You find me distasteful?"

Grayson stood as well and glared back at her. "Am I supposed to be enjoying your insults?"

"In response to yours?" she snapped back. "Take me home, please."

"With pleasure." He bent to grab the picnic basket and blanket. With long strides, he headed to the wagon, dragging the blanket behind him. "Come along. If we hurry, you can make it back in time for the people to catch a glimpse of us, as most may not have made it home by now."

He turned to see her rushing in the opposite direction, her arms pumping with each step. When she reached a tree, she rested her shoulder against it. Grayson wondered if he should go to her, but didn't trust himself not to say something else that would make things worse. Instead, he waited by the wagon, leaning against it, staring into the distance.

"I apologize." Nora had neared and he'd not heard her approach. The contrite expression on her face contrasted with the challenge in the golden brown pools of her eyes. "I should not have lowered myself to name calling."

Grayson shrugged, ignoring the jab in his chest at her lack of sincerity. "Sure. Are you ready?"

They arrived at her house about half an hour later and

Grayson climbed down and went to assist her. Nora's stiff hand accepted his and she avoided eye contact until reaching her door. "You should apologize as well."

"For?"

When she glared up at him, Grayson fought back a smile. "For calling me distasteful."

"Oh, that," he replied and frowned. "I called the situation distasteful, not you."

"Fine. Good day, Mr. Cole," she snapped and turned to the door.

Grayson leaned forward and spoke into her ear, his lips brushing the tip. "I don't find you distasteful in the least."

Nora let out a loud gasp and swung to face him. "I take back my apology."

"You can't do that." Grayson smirked, enjoying her discomfort. "I've already accepted it."

"Ugh." With a shove of her shoulder she pushed the door open. "Good day, Mr. Cole."

His fingertips to the rim of his hat, Grayson tipped his head forward. "I look forward to your company next Sunday, Miss Banks."

She kept her back to him. "Liar."

A wide smile curved his lips when he rode away from her small house. A picture of her beautiful, angry eyes filled his mind. Grayson dug an apple out of the basket and took a big bite. Although not the date he expected, he had not lied upon taking his leave.

He did look forward to the following Sunday.

Chapter Six

From where Mitch sat in the saloon, he could keep an eye on his horse and had a clear view across the street to the outer edge of the hotel where Olivia had entered earlier with her sister and another woman. Olivia's beauty never ceased to amaze him. The sight of her in a bright yellow dress that closely matched her golden curls—she was like a ray of sunshine.

"You gonna play or stare out the window all day?" Glenn Walters, his gambling associate, grumbled. "Maybe you hopin' someone will come help you with your game?" He placed two pair, queens high, on the table. "'Spose they didn't make it." The man chuckled when Mitch threw his cards down. It was a mistake not to pay attention when playing Walters. The man cheated any chance he got.

"What's got you so interested in what's going on out there?" Matthew Corson, his childhood friend, asked looking past him through the window. His eyes slid to Walters. "You might as well not play unless you just want to give more money away."

Before more cards were dealt, Mitch stood and moved closer to the bar. He leaned over and watched the bartender pour whiskey into two glasses. An old gold miner picked up one of the glasses and swallowed greedily. The bartender slid the other one to Mitch.

He watched the bleary-eyed miner put the glass down. The miner's head then fell forward until it rested on his chest. Mitch wondered if that would be him in the next few years. After all, he spent more time in the saloon than anywhere else.

Most mornings, he spent helping his father at the mercantile. In the afternoons, he had little to do. Some days, he'd clean the store and take inventory. Most of the time, his parents took care of everything. Mitch had too much time. Most people would not complain of such a thing, but the last thing he needed was idle time. His mind would inevitably go to his sister's attack the night, ten years earlier, when he'd insisted Nora go to a barn dance with him and they'd met the stranger on the ride home.

The stranger, a man who was about his age now, had stood by the side of the road. When they'd stopped to inquire if he needed help, he'd seen that both were young and too dumb to suspect he was dangerous. If only he'd paid more heed to the tingle at the back of his neck when the man's gaze lingered on Nora. Instead, when the man asked for Mitch to help him see about his horse's leg, Mitch had readily dismounted. A quick hit with the butt of his gun and Mitch had fallen like a log. He didn't remember the hits that came after. Nora said he attempted to fight back, but he'd barely held on before blacking out.

And Nora, instead of running, had remained, too scared to leave him. When he'd come to, he'd found his poor sister a few yards away in the woods.

"Another one, Mitch?" The bartender was already pouring a fresh drink, which he picked up and carried towards the window.

When Olivia emerged from the hotel, he locked on the sight of her. If ever there was a woman he'd gladly spend his life with, it was Olivia Dougherty. Time flew whenever he'd taken her on rides. Lost in her husky voice and soft laughter, he could spend endless hours listening to her talk. If only he could allow himself the luxury of a relationship. No, not until Nora was settled, would he consider a separate life of his own. His sister needed someone to look out for her. He'd failed her once and that was more than enough to motivate him to watch over her, even if it was for a lifetime.

Perhaps if things worked out between Grayson Cole and Nora, then he could think about courting Olivia. Just then, movement caught his eye and his gut clenched. Grayson Cole neared Olivia's group and they began to talk. Ire filled Mitch at seeing Olivia throw her head back and laugh at something the cad said. Mitch moved to the door to get a closer look. Grayson's hand reached for Olivia. He seemed to be offering to walk with her.

How dare the man not only openly flirt with Olivia, but at the same time disrespect his sister in such a manner? He must have growled out loud because Matthew came up beside him. "Somethin' wrong?"

Husky laughter sounded again and, without thought, Mitch threw himself through the swinging doors and sprinted across the street. Everything turned red. One person came into focus at the end of his tunneled vision. Grayson.

Mitch grabbed Grayson's shoulder and turned the man around. At the same time, he swung and punched Grayson's face. Grayson had no time to react and fell backward onto the sidewalk. Olivia and her party shrieked and scattered.

Mitch stood over the fallen man. "Get up, Grayson."

"Damn right I will." Grayson rushed to his feet and tackled Mitch around the waist. Both men fell onto the dirt road and began to wrestle. Mitch ignored the sound of footsteps and hollering. He lifted an arm to deflect Grayson's fist and rolled to his side, managing to get to his feet. Grayson swung again, connecting with Mitch's midsection and doubling him over with a loud "Umph."

"Get 'em up," Grayson growled.

Matthew landed on his butt at Mitch's feet. Matthew winked at Mitch before jumping to his feet and swinging at Bronson Cole, who'd come to help his brother. The sound of more scrambling caught his attention. Glenn Walters and Ashley Cole were now trading punches like two prizefighters. Mitch swung and connected with the side of Grayson's face. He went to swing again only to receive a hard punch to his own face.

A gunshot boomed; the startling sound made them stop.

The town sheriff, Miles Dawson, approached, his face a storm of anger. "One more swing and I'm taking you all to jail." The tall, lanky man came to stand next to Mitch. "All of you go on now and get out of here." He looked at Grayson and his brothers. "Get on home, boys. I'll speak to you later."

The twins went to leave, then as one they turned and went toward Ashley who'd not moved away from Glenn Walters. Both men stared at each other, animosity straining between them. Even after the twins grabbed Ashley, the man did not break eye contact. "This isn't over, Walters." His deep voice soft, but loud enough so that everyone heard it.

Finally, the brothers left and Mitch turned to find Sheriff Dawson studying him with a closed expression. "I'm not going to ask what that was all about. But I am going to tell you that I don't abide drunks picking fights in my town."

A drunk. Was that what he was now? Mitch held his handkerchief to his brow in an attempt to stop the blood from flowing into his eyes. "I apologize, Sheriff, it won't happen again."

"See to it. Next time you're going to jail." The man stuck out his chest when Olivia and her friend neared.

Eyes narrowed, Olivia's gaze roamed over him, her mouth pursed with disapproval. "Well, Mitch Banks, whatever has come over you? I don't know why you hit Grayson, but I assure you we did nothing more than speak of the weather." She shook her head and took a breath. "I am not sure what to think of your behavior."

"Ladies." Sheriff Dawson tipped his hat and interrupted before Mitch could answer. "Miss Dougherty, I believe it's best if Mitch sees your father. The cut over his eye is quite large. It may need a few stitches."

"I'll take care of it myself," Mitch replied. The last thing he needed right now was to go to Olivia's father's office. Doctor Dougherty, although mild mannered, was also overly protective of his daughter.

"Of course, Sheriff, you're right." Olivia slid Mitch another disapproving look then looked to Walter and Matthew who'd moved against the building as if hoping to become invisible. "Both of you need looked at, too. Come along. Bring him to father's." She turned on her heel and walked toward Doc Dougherty's office, which was a block away. Like sheep, the men followed without a word. Although young and beautiful, Olivia was also well known for her vibrant temper, doctoring abilities, and remarkable marksmanship.

Both Walter and Matthew were quickly patched up and dismissed, leaving Mitch last to be seen. He sat on a long, padded table and watched the doctor wash his hands. Olivia stood alongside where Mitch was seated, her nose raised just a hair higher than usual. She'd not spoken to him the entire time, instead kept busy assisting her father.

"Olivia, rinse out the gash before I stitch it up." Doc Dougherty nodded at a bowl of clean water. Mitch closed his eyes when she leaned closer and removed the cloth from his brow. The scent of fresh flowers surrounded him and he inhaled for more of it. Her hands were not gentle when she held his head and used a wet cloth to clean the wound, quite the opposite.

Mitch drew in breath sharply when she rubbed the wet cloth across it a fourth time. "Ouch."

"I think you require a bit of antiseptic," Olivia purred, her voice sweet. Mitch opened one eye and looked at her, but she turned his head so he could not see her. "Keep still."

The strong scent of the antiseptic should have warned him of what came next, but the sting of the foul liquid caught him unawares. He groaned through clenched teeth and attempted to jerk his head out of her hold, yet she managed to dab another bit of the painful treatment to a small cut on his lip. "Ouch." Mitch lowered one leg from the table when the doctor stepped in and pushed him back to sit.

"Olivia, you didn't have to use quite that much. No wonder Mitch was squealing." The doctor shook his head. "Are you all right, Mitch?"

His pride stung almost as much as the antiseptic. "Yes, sir, I'm fine."

Doctor Dougherty chuckled. "At least we don't have to worry about an infection. Now close your eyes so I can get this cut stitched. It won't be but a bit."

Perhaps to distract him, the doc began to talk. "Yep, in my day, we fought over most anything. I remember once the old sheriff threw my brothers and me in jail when we got into a fistfight during a town festival. Ended up in there 'til our Pa paid for all the damage we did 'cause we tore up the sheriff's wife's display of pottery." The man shook his head. "I don't know what you and those boys fought about, but I will tell ya, those Cole brothers are good fighters and it looks like you held your own."

A few minutes later, his head throbbing, Mitch made his way out of the doctor's office. Olivia was nowhere in sight. He wasn't sure when, but sometime while her father stitched him up, she'd left. He wanted to be relieved at her absence, but disappointment nudged that thought out of the way.

Now, to face his sister and find out if she had already heard what happened.

Chapter Seven

"Ouch, Ma," Grayson groaned when the needle poked through his skin. "That stings."

"It should teach you not to get into fights. My goodness, at your age this makes two incredibly stupid things you've done in the last couple weeks," his mother admonished while glaring around the room at his brothers. "All of you know better than to make a spectacle of yourselves in town, in the middle of the day no less."

"Mitch Banks attacked Grayson. We simply stepped in when his two friends went after him, too," Ashley explained, shocking everyone in the room with the longest remark he'd made in a long time.

"Why did Mitch hit you?" his mother asked. "It doesn't sound like him."

"I don't know. I was talking to Olivia Dougherty and the next thing I knew, he swung me around and hit me." Grayson grimaced when the needle poked again.

"If he's sweet on Olivia, I'm sure he suspected you were attempting to seduce the girl, or being disrespectful of his sister."

"It was neither," Grayson grumbled. "The man was drunk."

Finally, his mother finished and he remained sitting, a

mug of coffee in his hands. Ashley followed her out while Bronson remained in the room, his eyes on the doorway as if he, too, wanted to leave. But he was forced to stay put since his mother told him to sit tight and keep an eye on her stew. Grayson looked up at his brother. "Why have you been so quiet? You barely speak to me. Am I offending everyone these days?"

"Why her?" The question meant nothing to Grayson. But seeing the darkness of Bronson's expression, Grayson decided it was best to wait before answering.

Darkened blue eyes met his. "You can have any woman in Alder Gulch. You've had half of them. Why Nora Banks?"

"Why Nora Banks what?" His already pounding head pulsed. "I didn't ask for any of this. What the heck are you asking me?"

"Nora," Bronson replied as if that answered anything. "She deserves more. Someone who actually cares for her. Not you, who sees her as a bother."

"I don't see her as a bother," Grayson snapped. "And just so you know, neither of us are thrilled with the current circumstances."

Bronson bent lower so his face was right in front of Grayson's, almost nose-to-nose. "Are you sure about that?" He straightened and ran his fingers through his short hair. "Watch Ma's stew, I need to get away from you."

Confused and aching, Grayson let his head fall back. "What the hell just happened?" he muttered.

"Mind your mouth, boy." His father walked into the kitchen. Hank Cole went to the stove and poked a spoon into the pot giving it a quick stir before picking up the coffee pot and pouring some dark liquid into a cup. "Who are you talking to anyway?"

"Bronson's mad at me. Ma's not too pleased with me either and, for some reason, Mitch Banks found it necessary to redecorate my face with his fists. I am not sure what I did, but I've got everyone riled up and angry."

His father sat down at the table and took a drink of coffee before he looked to Grayson. "Your Ma is upset that her baby got hurt. She's not mad at you. As for Mitch Banks, well, only he knows what spurred him to do this. You and your brother? Now, that one you need to work out. Talk to him."

It took him a bit to stand from the chair. The ache, now a dull throb, was easier to ignore, so Grayson went in search of Bronson. After wandering through the house, Grayson found his twin in the barn. Brushing his horse down, Bronson visibly tensed at Grayson's presence, but ignored him.

"Why are you mad about Nora?"

Bronson shrugged. "You don't know?"

His stomach sunk at realizing that perhaps Nora and Bronson were courting and he wasn't aware. "Was Nora waiting for you in the hayloft?"

There was no expression in Bronson's face when he turned to look at Grayson. "No."

"Then what?"

"I'd asked her father for permission to court her just before the festival." Bronson threw down the brush and walked past him out of the barn toward the house.

Grayson could only gawk at his brother's back. Beyond Bronson, a buggy pulled up at the house. Nora.

Not good timing.

The entire ride out, Nora practiced what she'd say to Grayson. If the man was already making a fool out of her by continuing his attempts to dally with other women, then she wanted no part of continuing the farce of their relationship. Her plan was set. Go straight to him and tell him she never wanted to see him again. No need for conversation or any type of apology.

She climbed down from the buggy and glanced toward the house. It would be bad etiquette not to speak to

Elizabeth Cole first. Footsteps neared and she turned to see Bronson advancing. Nora steeled herself against softening. Right now, she needed to stay angry.

"Good afternoon, Nora." Bronson looked at her. He then shifted his gaze over to the house. "Grayson's not in the house, he's in the barn."

"I'm sorry," Nora blurted. "I know you spoke to my father. I planned to talk to you. I should have spoken to you about all this." She motioned to the barn. "You intended on courting me and I..."

"I did." His statement was even and his eyes flat. "But looks like things worked out differently."

"I wouldn't have accepted." Nora couldn't believe how blunt her words sounded, but she'd come planning to get things straight between her and the Cole brothers.

Finally, Bronson showed emotion, his brows drawing together. "Why?"

This was not the time to pull any punches. "I admire you, Bronson, I really do. You are definitely the better choice. But you look too much..."

"I look just like him. After all, we are twins," he finished through clenched teeth and looked over his shoulder towards the barn. "Does he know how you feel?"

Her heart thumped against her breastbone. "No. I'm not sure it matters anyway. I came to make sure the farce of our relationship ends."

Bronson's shoulders fell and his entire countenance softened. "He's not a bad man, Nora. Just afraid." Without another word, he went past her to the house and entered, closing the door behind him.

Picking up her skirts to keep them from dragging, Nora made her way to the barn. Of course, Bronson would defend his twin. But he knew as much as she did, Grayson was not the settling kind.

Once inside the barn, it took a few minutes for her eyes to grow accustomed to the dimness of the interior. When she could see, her first instinct was to look up to the hayloft. Her cheeks warmed at the remembrance of what happened only two weeks earlier. Instantly, she remembered the feel of the warmth and hardness of Grayson's body when he'd fallen on top of her. Annoyed at the direction her thoughts went, Nora stalked from the front of the building and continued past empty stalls only to realize Grayson was nowhere inside.

Once past the last stall, she ventured through to the other side of the barn where the corrals stood. Several large, beautiful horses grazed lazily in the late afternoon sun while others pranced as if putting on a show.

On the side of the building, sitting on an upside down bucket, was Grayson. He'd not heard her. Shoulders slumped and hands with fingers entwined on his lap, Grayson sat with his chin resting on his chest. Even though he was obviously upset and had his guard down, his muscular physique was a thing of beauty. His shoulder-length hair shielded his face and Nora vacillated whether to go to him or leave.

She approached and placed her hand on his wide shoulder. He did not move or acknowledge her presence. "Grayson?"

His next action took her by surprise. His calloused hand covered hers. "Don't say whatever you plan to say. You're probably mad at me, too, just like everyone else. Let me just apologize for everything that I've ever done to you and everyone." Finally, he lifted his face to her. Bewilderment displayed in his eyes when they met hers. His brows drawn together, he attempted to smile, but failed. An angry, swollen gash above his left eye had been stitched and his split bottom lip was now purpled and healing. Nora stepped away, not sure she could keep from wrapping her arms around his shoulders, comforting him.

Grayson stood and began to pace. His head was still down. He ran his fingers through his hair, combing it from his face. Jaw hard, he looked at her for a moment before speaking. "I am not sure what I did today that upset your brother. It seems that no matter what I do, everyone assumes the worst of me. I suppose that's why no one believed us about the hayloft incident. I'm trying to figure out how to get out of this, Nora, without you being affected."

He took a breath and went back to the bucket and sat. "Now my brother's mad at me. I'm not sure what to do about that yet. Guess I'll figure that out, too."

His pain rattled her. She'd never considered that all his bravado was nothing more than a façade.

"It will work out, you'll see." When she placed her hand on his shoulder again, he slid from under it and stood. Not stepping from her, they stood close. He looked down at her, his eyes searching her face as if she held an answer to all his problems. Nora placed her hands gingerly on both sides of his face and drew him down to her. His eyes widened for a moment before closing. She pressed her lips against his and feathered soft kisses from one end of his mouth to the other, careful not to hurt him.

Grayson responded and tilted his head and kissed her back, his eyes still closed. Nothing could tear her away from him when he relaxed against her, his large, firm body sagging. His arms went around her, continuing to take her mouth with his. A soft sound hummed from his throat.

Nora ran her fingers through his silky hair and parted her lips, allowing the beautiful invasion of his tongue. He tasted of smoke and peril but she'd die before pulling away from the precipice that was Grayson Cole. Everything she dreamed of, how he'd feel, taste, and sound, sank into her being and she relished the warmth of his embrace. His lips began to trail from her mouth and she lifted her face to give him more access. "Nora." The simple whisper asked permission to move forward and her moaned response of his name granted it.

She slid her hands down his back and urged him forward, needing more closeness. Her body demanded it. Grayson's soft exhalation against her throat followed by his hot tongue swirling on the surface of her skin drove her to gasp loudly.

The stark sound of a throat clearing broke the spell.

Shocked, Nora pushed from Grayson and stumbled back from him. She jerked her head over to see Ashley standing at the barn entrance. Eyebrows raised, his midnight blue eyes went from her to Grayson and back. "Ma's coming."

Grayson also cleared his throat and ran both hands through his hair in an attempt to settle the tresses from the tousled mess she'd created. Nora would have laughed at his discomfort if she'd not been busy patting her own down.

The older brother disappeared into the barn, and she heard the low rumble of his voice followed by Elizabeth Cole's animated reply and laughter. God, had he told her what he'd seen?

Nora glanced to Grayson. He'd moved away and held a hand out to a horse that'd neared him. He seemed totally at ease, as if the moment between them had never happened. Of course, the prospect of his mother's appearance could be the explanation, but for some insane reason, Nora felt affronted at his nonchalance.

"There you are." Elizabeth exited the barn, a warm smile on her lips. She glanced at Grayson but did not speak to him. "Why don't you join me for a cup of tea, Nora?"

"I'm sorry for my lack of manners in not coming in to see you before coming to speak to Grayson." Nora went to the woman and hugged her. "It's just that I was upset over the fight."

"Say no more," Grayson's mother replied with a quick look in Grayson's direction before threading her arm through Nora's. "How is your brother?"

"About the same as him," Nora replied looking over to Grayson who continued to keep his back to them. "Or maybe a bit worse."

They meandered toward the house and, by Elizabeth's pursed lips, Nora braced for what the woman would say.

"I know this is difficult, Nora," she began. "It's hard on Gray as well. I'm not sure what you and he spoke of just now, but I want to urge you to give this situation plenty of thought. I don't agree with a forced marriage, of course, and I don't want either of you to get hurt. Especially my son." Worry-filled eyes met Nora's. "He's been through enough heartache although I think this may be the only way for him to finally have what he needs; a wife and a family. I also don't want both of you to be miserable."

Nora could only nod in silence.

Elizabeth took a deep breath and smiled at her. "If you could care for my son enough to give him the opportunity, he'll prove to be a good man and faithful husband. I know it's hard to believe, but that tough, rake exterior is just his way of protecting himself."

His mother, of course, saw the best in Grayson and although Nora expected that some of what she Elizabeth was true, she had a hard time believing that Grayson Cole could ever be faithful.

Chapter Eight

That was the best kiss he'd ever experienced. Grayson stood frozen, facing the horse that nuzzled his extended hand. He'd turned away when his mother approached to keep from embarrassing himself. His arousal pressed inside his britches and he adjusted his stance. He trembled. God, when was the last time he'd been affected so much from a simple kiss?

Pliable and supple under his hands, her curves fit perfectly against his body. He'd no idea why she'd come, as he'd not given her an opportunity to speak. Instead, he'd gone on spilling his guts. Still thinking about Bronson's confession, she'd caught him at a rotten time.

Sophia's face appeared in his mind's eye and, instantly, guilt assailed him. Grayson doubled over against the fence, not able to breathe past the heaviness in his chest. "I'm so sorry." He clutched at the wooden gate and attempted to keep from falling when his legs almost gave out. "I'm so sorry." His voice shook.

Ashley approached and leaned against the fence next to him. "Breathe through it, Gray. It's all right."

The calmness in Ashley's voice like a soothing balm. It had an instant influence and the panic subsided, his breathing easier.

"You gonna go see about your fiancée?"

Grayson slid him a glare. "And do what?"

His brother shrugged. "Don't know, sit and talk I guess."

"I can't, Ash. I can't do it. My lip is throbbing. I need a drink."

"I got some whiskey at the bunkhouse."

They walked alongside each other in silence, which was usual when spending time with Ashley. Ashley lived in the bunkhouse alone, except when the ranch hands stayed during breeding season and harvesting. Just after returning from his time in the cavalry, he'd moved out when his nightmares caused his parents to worry and the family to wake at his screams. Although Elizabeth fought him on it, Ashley insisted he needed space. Everyone suspected it was his way to keep them from experiencing sleepless nights.

They entered the bunkhouse and Ashley brought a bottle of whiskey from a shelf to the table and poured them both a drink. Grayson swallowed the burning liquid and instantly felt its effect. Not a drinker, he preferred to keep away from liquor. The instant response from his gut was to lurch in protest.

"Thank you. It helps," he told Ashley, holding his glass out for a refill.

"I can see that," Ashley responded with a shake of his head. "You sure?"

"Yeah." Grayson watched the liquid in his glass. "Bronson is angry with me."

"He'll get over it," Ashley replied, swirling the whiskey in his own cup and watching the liquid closely. "Don't know what he wants yet."

"He wants Nora."

"She's not meant for him." Grayson studied his sullen brother. There was barely a bruise on his face. With dark hair their mother kept short, he wore a mustache and trim beard, which made his dark blue eyes stand out. He was taller than Grayson and Bronson by at least two inches and broader. The enormous male preferred a solitary life, spending most of his days herding and doing repairs to the perimeter of the fencing. His mother insisted he join the family for dinner every day, but that only meant he showed up, at most, twice a week.

"What do you do most evenings, Ash?"

"Most days, I'm too tired from work to clean up and come to dinner with y'all. Cook does a good job of feeding us during the day. If I'm planning to stay here, I grab some extra bread or something easy and eat that."

"Right." Grayson looked around the space. In addition to two leather bound books, a knife and shaving stuff on a crude shelf, there were a couple of blankets rolled on his bunk. Several shirts and a jacket hung from pegs on the wall. Pants were neatly folded on top of a trunk. Next to the pants were an extra pair of boots. His brother lived simply. "I don't see you much. I'd like to spend more time with you." His words slurred and Ashley lifted an eyebrow.

"You spend most of your day looking after the horses. Keeps you from fieldwork where I'm at. Have you eaten today?"

Swallowing the last of the whiskey, Grayson shook his head. His eyes became heavy and he blinked, attempting to open them wider. "No. I ain't hungry. I better go and see 'bout Nora."

When Grayson stood, the room tilted and he would have fallen if not for Ashley grabbing his arm. "You need to lay down. After the fight and not eating, the liquor is about to put you out."

"I'm all right, just tired." Grayson tried to move away, but his head fell onto Ashley's shoulder.

"Yeah, maybe I do need to rest a bit."

The sun was setting when Grayson woke. An oil lamp lit the empty bunkhouse and he sat up and looked around.

With a wide yawn, he stood and stretched, feeling rested. He eyed the whiskey bottle. Perhaps liquor wasn't all that bad, especially if it allowed for rest when his mind was so full that he'd probably spend most of the night fretting over Bronson, Nora and Mitch Banks.

Raindrops began to fall and thunder sounded in the distance. From the bunkhouse, he walked towards his parents' house. Angry, grey clouds moved in and the wind picked up. Light poured from every window and he climbed the steps to the front door. Once inside, his mother's high-toned voice sounding from the kitchen stopped him.

"What has gotten in to you boys, out there fighting like outlaws? Running wild, acting more like children than adults."

Grayson tiptoed past the doorway and headed for the stairs. Luck was with him. Ashley and Bronson could get the tongue lashing without him.

When his mother spoke again, he stopped and listened. "Poor Nora is beside herself with worry. Her brother attacking Grayson and all, the girl has been through enough without having to worry about Mitch and Grayson brawling in the street."

"Like you said, Ma, Mitch attacked first. When his friends jumped in, me and Ash couldn't just stand there," Bronson's low voice rumbled in reply.

Grayson escaped to his room and lay on the bed. His stomach growled, but it would wait 'til morning. He wasn't about to go downstairs and face his angry mother.

What had Nora said to his mother? How long had she stayed and visited? He wondered if his mother was aware of what happened between them prior to her coming out to the barn. Most likely, she'd been able to tell from Nora's flushed face and kiss-swollen lips. He closed his eyes and thought about the woman he was supposed to marry. It would be so easy to just let go and allow the circumstances free reign. But at the same time, it would be too easy to develop feelings for her and open himself to pain.

The thought of it brought a physical ache in his chest and Grayson sat up, attempting to catch his breath. It took him long months just to wake up and face the day without first having to push past the pain of his loss after Sophia died. No, he wouldn't do it. He chose not to take that type of risk again.

Besides, he couldn't hurt Bronson that way. Regardless of whether he ended up with Nora or not, it would be hard for his brother to see her regularly as sister-in-law. Heck, he wasn't sure if seeing her would be much easier for him after what they'd shared.

Two days later, it continued raining. The water pelted the roof of the barn and Grayson looked up to ensure none of it leaked in before moving to the next stall. The horses seemed calm regardless of the ruckus outside.

"Grayson!" Bronson rushed in, his wet hair plastered to his head. "The sheriff arrested Ashley."

"When?"

"I reckon yesterday when he went to town to pick up provisions for the bunkhouse. One of the ranch hands, Josiah, came and told Pa after he went to check on him." Bronson took a breath. "They say he killed Glenn Walters."

"Is Pa going to town?"

"He asked that you and I go. He's staying, worried about the rain. The river is high and may overrun."

"I'll go. You stay here and help in case it does." Grayson was already tightening the saddle straps on his horse. "I'll find out what can be done after I get some cash from the strongbox. I'll stay in town until Ash is freed."

Bronson nodded and looked toward the house. "Maybe I should go with you. I mean, it is a wicked storm out there. But Pa will need help if the river does flood."

"That's why you need to stay here." Grayson was glad

that his brother no longer seemed angry with him. "I'll be fine."

The twins arrived at the house. Their father was comforting their mother. She looked up at Grayson and sniffed. "This is horrible. Ashley did no such thing. He's been here since you all got back from town two days ago. Miles just doesn't like him."

Grayson went to his mother and rubbed her arm. "Don't worry, Ma, I'm gonna go see about Ashley. I'll take care of things."

Hank followed Grayson to the office, his face a mixture of outrage and concern. "Go see Archie Wade. Hire the attorney and tell him to get Ash out of that place."

"I will, Pa."

The trip to town took longer than expected. At times, he could barely see past his nose thanks to the deluge. He shivered from the cold, his jacket soaked through, but he continued until reaching the sheriff's office.

Grayson walked in without knocking. Inside, the sheriff's deputy sat at a ramshackle desk, his boots up and his hands behind his head. The man's bored gaze met Grayson's and then looked past him. "Surprised you came by yourself. You Coles rarely travel alone."

"Where's my brother?" He had no time to waste on swapping insults with the man. "I want to see him."

"Mind your manners, son." The man didn't budge from his relaxed position, but his body tensed. "You come in here, you don't demand anything."

Grayson sighed and looked toward the short hallway, which he knew led to the cells. It worried him that Ashley had not responded and let him know he was all right. But, then again, his brother rarely spoke around others. "I'd like to see my brother, Deputy."

"See now, it don't hurt to be respectful." The deputy unfolded from the chair, picked up a heavy key ring, and motioned for Grayson to precede him into the next room. Grayson caught sight of Ashley. His brother lay on a hard bunk, his hands pillowing his head, staring up at the ceiling. Grayson looked to the deputy. "What kind of proof you got?"

"He threatened Walters in front of the sheriff. What more you want?"

"That isn't proof he did anything," Grayson snapped. Ashley sat up and watched the exchange, his eyes locked on the deputy.

The man shifted from one foot to the other, obviously discomfited by Ashley's unblinking regard. "Look, you need to talk to Sheriff Dawson. It's up to him. He just went to see about his family and should be back in an hour or two."

"I'd like to spend a few minutes talking to Ashley." Grayson eyed the keys. "You can lock me up with him for now if you wish."

The deputy motioned to Ashley. "Get back in the corner, turn your back, and put your hands up behind your head while I unlock this here door and put your brother in."

Ashley rolled his eyes, but did as the deputy bid. Grayson held his breath hoping his brother remained in the corner. He had no doubt Ashley could escape if he wanted to.

Once the deputy locked the door, he eyed them with more bravado. "You got fifteen minutes."

Grayson stalked to the cell door almost smiling when the smaller man moved back. "Since when is there a time limit?"

"I ain't got to explain nothin' to ya." The deputy's eyes shifted to the front office, someone had entered. "Just holler when you're done."

"How are you holding up?" Grayson asked Ashley who'd sat on the bunk and leaned against the wall. "Ma is right upset about this. Pa and Bronson didn't come because the rain is making the river rise pretty high."

Ashley's gaze shifted to the doorway. "I ain't worried. I didn't do it." He placed his hands beside his legs and looked down. "I hate not being able to help at the ranch if the river overflows."

Grayson remained standing, too wet to sit on the bed. "I don't believe it will." It would be bad for it to happen with both him and Ashley not there.

"You don't need to get Wade. Just wait until the sheriff gets talking to people and he'll find out I didn't do it, soon enough."

"That could take a week or more, Ash. You know Uncle Miles doesn't like you. Ma will come here and throw a fit on his head if you have to stay here much longer."

Ashley's chuckle rumbled from his chest. "Wouldn't want to be Dawson if she decides to do that." He eyed Grayson's clothes. "You're soaked. You need to get somewhere and get out of those clothes before you get sick."

"Here." Grayson handed Ashley a bundle that he'd managed to keep dry. "Ma insisted I bring this. It's some dried beef and what not."

"You're shivering," Ashley told him reaching for the bundle. "Go on now, I'll be all right. 'Spose you can stop by the brothel and ask for dry clothes. Sometimes they got some."

Grayson wasn't sure he wanted to know how Ashley knew this. "All right. I got a couple things to do for Pa. I'll be back in the morning."

With one hand on Ashley's shoulder Grayson called for the deputy.

Grayson found himself standing on Nora's porch, his fist about to connect with the door. A shiver shot through him and he wondered if he wasn't already sick from wearing the soaking wet clothing. He'd housed his horse at the stables and walked the short distance to her house. Not sure what to expect, actually the slamming of the door in his face would not surprise him in the least, he knocked. After two pounds on the door, he called out. "Nora, it's me, Grayson."

The door opened, warm air hitting his frozen face. Brows drawn and lips slightly parted, she looked up at him. "Grayson, what in the world are you thinking?" Nora took a step back and opened the door further. "You're soaked to the skin, you fool."

If his teeth were not rattling, he'd have laughed. Instead, he scurried to stand in front of the fireplace and tore off his jacket. It fell with a plop on the floor. "I'm sorry...had to come...see about my b-brother." He got as close as he could to the fire and stuck his hands out to the warmth.

"I'll get you some dry clothes," Nora said and he heard her retreating footsteps. Just like her to take care of things first. He began to unbutton his shirt, a task that proved hard with shaky fingers.

Nora returned with what looked like flannel pants and a heavy work shirt. "Here, these are Mitch's. You can undress. I'll be in the kitchen heating water for tea."

"Thank you." Grayson swallowed at noticing she wore only a nightgown. Thankfully, it was thick. Unfortunately, it still made him think of her in bed. "I'll hang my wet clothes on the hooks here to let them dry."

"See that you do," she told him and left the room.

A few minutes later, finally in dry clothes, warmth seeped into his cold body. He remained by the fire not wanting to move away from the heat.

"Here, drink this." Nora held out a steaming mug that he grabbed with eagerness. The warmness of it was a welcome feel. "It's tea with a bit of whiskey."

"I'm sorry to come here uninvited," he began and took a sip of the hot liquid. "A family problem needed taken care of."

She glanced toward the door. "You came alone in this weather?" After placing a new log in the fireplace, she sat.

Grayson nodded and followed her lead, sitting across from her in a comfortable chair close enough to the fireplace that he still felt the warmth of the fire. "Yes. My brother, Ashley, is in jail. Sheriff Dawson is holding him because Walters is dead."

"I see," Nora replied with a frown. "Is Ashley all right?"

His shoulder muscles relaxed at her lack of judgment of his brother. "Seems to be. It's hard to tell with Ashley."

"He's a quiet one, isn't he?" Her eyes met his for a second and then went to the fire. "I've never really gotten to know him. I hear that he doesn't talk much to anyone but family."

"My brother hasn't been the same since he came back from the service, but he's not a bad person. He did not kill that man. Not once has he left the ranch in the last few days, especially since we had that tussle with your brother and his friends."

"Glenn Walters could hardly be qualified as a friend of Mitch's. The only reason he joined in the fight was probably because he was aiming to ingratiate himself with Mitch."

"Well, something he did got him killed."

"What are you going to do about Ashley?" Her eyes met his again and before he could help it, he looked to her lips. She pressed them together and turned away.

"I'm going to see Mr. Wade in the morning, hire him to get Ashley out."

"Good." Nora placed her cup on a side table, stood and moved to the fireplace. "Why did you come here tonight?" Her question was quiet.

He stared at her profile and couldn't help admiring the perfectly shaped nose, long lashes, and pert chin. "I suppose I needed to know if you're still angry with me over the fight."

"Yeah, I am. I'm not sure why I'm angry with you. It's not like I expect faithfulness from this farce of an engagement. I just didn't think you'd be so open about it."

Grayson wasn't sure what else to say and he wondered what he'd do next. The rain outside continued to fall with gusto and he eyed the window and wondered if it would lighten up so he'd not get soaked again going to the hotel. "It was Olivia and her lady friends that struck up the conversation. All we discussed was the weather. Next thing I know, your brother is decking me."

Her honey brown eyes met his, her face peaceful. Grayson stood and went to her. He neared with caution, looking for any sign that she did not welcome his proximity. They maintained eye contact and Nora did not step away from him. "I believe you, Grayson. I'm not sure why, but I do."

"That's all I ask," he replied, his voice husky. "Thank you for opening the door for me. I just needed to talk to someone. Can I kiss you, Nora?"

Eyes widening, her nod followed. He took her mouth. The softness of Nora's lips immediately sent a surge of want through him. Thoughts of how wonderful her body felt against him tore into his mind and Grayson pulled her into his arms. He pressed a trail of kisses from her mouth to her ear. "I can't get out of my mind, how you feel against me, your taste, your soft body in my arms. You affect me like no one ever has."

Nora inhaled sharply and laid her head on his chest. "That, I do find hard to believe."

Grayson took her mouth again, hungry for more of what he knew was a banquet of desire. When her arms went around his neck, delight struck him senseless.

She'd wanted a kiss from the moment she'd opened the door for him. Even soaking wet and shivering, he sent her heart to thumping so hard she feared he heard it. When he'd been changing, she peeked in to see him nude before the fire. Never would she forget the beauty of his muscular body, the bunching of muscles when he'd pulled the wet clothes off. Thankfully, she'd placed her hand over her mouth when Grayson pulled off his pants. His legs were well formed, his butt even more so. Red-faced at her actions, she retreated into the kitchen, while at the same time wanting to look again, touch every inch of his tanned skin.

Now, as he kissed her with what she could only describe as hunger, Nora clung to him not wanting him to move away from her. "Grayson," she whispered between kisses. "You need to leave." She pushed into him and ran her hands down his back pulling him closer.

"Yes, I should leave." Grayson licked her neck to the top of her breast and pressed kissed across the sensitive skin. Nora shivered, a moan escaping before she could stop it. *Don't leave.*

"What?" He continued kissing across her breasts while his hand roamed down her back to cup her bottom. Oh God, she'd spoken out loud.

Nora placed her hands on both sides of his face and pulled him up to face her. Dazed blue eyes looked into hers, but he did not speak, only stared at her with a heated look.

"I don't want you to leave, Grayson. Not tonight."

A gasp escaped at the ardor by which he took her mouth. He was not gentle and every inch of her body reacted. She grabbed at him, her nails digging into the rough fabric.

Grayson stepped away from her, his breathing ragged. "I'll sleep on the floor in here, if that's all right."

Embarrassed that she would have allowed things to progress between them, she wrapped her arms around her waist and looked to the fire, the flames mimicking the heat of her body.

"Come to me." Grayson seemed to know her mind was going elsewhere. He took her hand and brought her against him. "Look at me, Nora."

And she did, Nora dove into the pools of blue and

pressed against him, her breasts flattening against the hard planes of his chest.

"I would never take advantage of you allowing me inside your home. But I don't want to stop kissing you. Let me."

Nora rose to her toes and placed a kiss on his throat.

He reacted with a sharp inhalation. "You're not playing fair." The hoarseness in his voice made her smile.

He kissed her again and sped up the motions and without further prompting, her world shattered.

In a daze she became lost in him, never wanting the kisses to end. Finally, he pulled back and his eyes bore into hers. "I've wanted to kiss you for so long."

He helped her to the floor. Grayson leaned on a large chair and pulled Nora to sit beside him, both looking into the fire.

The fire was losing its warmth and Grayson put another log on top of the embers. He grabbed a blanket from the chair and joined her on the floor again.

He pressed kisses on her temples and lips, his eyes searching her face. "Please don't tell me you're sorry this happened. That we kissed like this." He cupped her chin and pressed his lips against hers.

Shocked at his words, Nora looked up at him. "Of course I'm not."

"Good, because we're engaged, so there's nothing to be sorry for anyhow." He frowned and let out a resigned breath.

A chuckle escaped her and he gave her a questioning look, brows drawn over his beautiful eyes.

Nora traced her finger down his straight nose and peered up at him. "We're still not getting married, Grayson. I know you don't want to marry me and I've accepted that I am not destined to be a wife."

"What are you saying? You don't want to marry me?"

"*You* don't want to marry me."

"I don't want to marry anyone, not just you," he replied

pulling her head back onto his chest. "It was true what I said, though."

"About?"

"I've desired you for a long time. Just kept my distance because I was afraid of how you affect me."

Nora did not reply. She wondered what he meant, but it didn't matter. They were not meant to be.

"Kiss me again," she whispered.

Grayson's mouth took hers and he pulled her against his broad chest. His hands traveled down her sides while his mouth plundered.

Just as she relaxed against him, preparing to take more from him, continue the delicious explorations, she realized he'd called her by the wrong name.

"Sophia."

Chapter Nine

"I'll get Ashley out by this afternoon," Archie Wade exclaimed pointing at Grayson. "Sounds like Sheriff Dawson doesn't have any proof. He has to let him go."

"My brother threatened Walters two days prior in front of the sheriff, the deputy and half the town."

"Your brother is well known for that temper of his. His demeanor doesn't help things either. But I stand on my word." The rotund man stood and rounded his desk. "I'll go down there right now." He eyed Grayson, reaching for his hat. "Alone. It's best if I go by myself. You look ready to kill someone and that won't be helpful for Ashley."

"If you need to talk to my brother, he may not talk if I'm not there."

Archie Wade nodded. "Then stay around town. If that happens, I'll come find you."

Not sure he trusted Wade alone with his brother, Grayson found himself in the shadowy interior of Stover's Saloon where he could be at the jailhouse within minutes. He shook his head when the bartender offered a drink. Instead, he finished the last of his coffee. Not sure if he could hold his temper in check as it was, a drink was a bad idea. He eyed Mitch and Matthew sitting across the room, each with a drink in hand. They pretended not to notice him.

That morning, he awoke to find Nora gone. Of course, classes started early and she'd left to ensure the children found the schoolhouse open. Yet, he'd been disappointed at not waking to see her. Although the thought of how much her absence affected him bothered Grayson, he couldn't shake the feeling. She left him a note instructing him to leave the key under the flowerpot on the front porch. No mention of expectations, or whether she enjoyed their time together. Both a first for him.

Part of him wanted to wait around for her and find out the answer to both questions. Did she really expect nothing from him? Was it possible for her to just walk away and not demand anything? She'd gotten up abruptly after kissing and bid him good night. Probably a good idea. As it was, he wasn't sure he could have kept from taking things further.

"How you doing, Grayson?" Lizzie, one of the saloon girls, leaned on the bar and smiled up at him. "How's Ashley doing?"

Grayson motioned for the bartender to serve Lizzie what was surely sugared water. "My brother is locked up for something he didn't do. I would say he's not doing too well."

"It's a shame." She took a sip of her drink. "I like Ashley."

The comment surprised him, but he didn't say anything about it. He decided it was best to try to find whatever information he could in regards to the dead man. "When was the last time you saw Walters here?"

She glanced around the saloon, scanning the room at leisure. "Can we go outside? I need some fresh air."

They walked out together. He felt Mitch's heated gaze on him and ignored it. The prostitute sashayed to the side of the building, her vibrant red dress standing out against the weathered exterior of the saloon. Lizzie smiled and looked up at the sky. "It's finally clearing up." The young woman's entire demeanor changed to more relaxed. Her freckles were obvious in the sunlight. It reminded him that she was someone's sister or daughter. Grayson dug his hands in his pockets and waited for her to talk.

"Walters was here that day, the day he was killed, two days ago." Lizzie shivered, an exaggerated motion, her auburn curls bouncing. "A mean man, that one. The girls he chose said he was rough, too. Poor Annabelle, he seemed to be drawn to her."

Grayson reeled her back. "Anything unusual happen while he was here?"

"Not for him. He got in an argument with a stranger who claimed he cheated at cards. Of course, with Walters, it was probably true." Lizzie huffed and looked back toward the front of the saloon. "I better go back inside."

"Wait," Grayson said as he placed a hand on her arm. "This stranger, did you tell Sheriff Dawson about him? Has he been back?"

Lizzie's head bobbed up and down. "Yes, I told the sheriff about it. He also asked for a description. The man came back last night, but didn't stay long. He's older, grey hair, long beard. Wears a miner's hat."

Grayson left from outside the saloon and headed for the sheriff's office. Once again, he found the deputy at the front desk, but this time he heard Sheriff Dawson's voice coming from the other room. He walked past the deputy who narrowed his eyes, but did not say anything.

Dawson sat outside Ashley's cell. A cup of coffee in hand, the man leaned forward staring at Ashley. His eyes slid to Grayson and back to Ashley. "Well good thing you're here. Maybe you can get your brother to talk. He ain't helpin' things none by playing this mute game."

"What do you need to know, Sheriff?" Grayson eyed his brother who sat on his bunk leaning against the wall, seeming relaxed. Ashley lifted an eyebrow. "He wants to know where I was night before last. I told him at home. He doesn't believe me. There's nothing else to say."

"Need to know who can verify he was at the ranch," Sheriff Dawson told Grayson. "Can't be family."

"The ranch hand, Josiah, and Ashley have been working getting the cattle rounded up and into the new corrals," Grayson replied, his eyes locked on to the sheriff. "Ashley even took care of me when I became sick and I slept in the bunkhouse the other night."

"He could have come here and killed Walters while you slept." The sheriff was being stubborn. Grayson knew it.

"I hear Walters got into an argument with a stranger the day he died. Have you checked into that, Dawson?"

At once on his feet, the sheriff closed the distance between them. "Tellin' me how to do my job, son?"

"Seems strange to me how you're spending so much time looking to make Ashley guilty, when the real killer is getting away." Grayson didn't back down. He held his ground. "Has Archie Wade been here?"

Ashley cleared his throat. "Yep, the sheriff refused to let me go."

"I told Wade to give it another day," Sheriff Dawson snapped.

"Instead of wasting time, I'm going to find this stranger." Grayson stormed from the building only to have Sheriff Dawson call to him from the door.

"Don't go and do something rash, Grayson. It's my job to find the culprit. Don't want to lock you up with your brother."

Grayson whirled and rushed back to the man who took a step back. "Don't look like you're trying very hard to do much other than keep my brother in jail."

"He's a danger to this town. You Coles refuse to see that, but I see the look in his eyes. He's killed before. He will probably kill again."

"He's your nephew. Why do you hate him so?"

"I am the law in this town. Whether family or not, I am fair."

"That is a bald-faced lie." Grayson stalked away.

Mitch wondered where Grayson was headed. After walking out with the saloon girl, only Lizzie returned. He eyed Matthew, who picked at a chip in the wooden tabletop. His friend seemed to be lost in thought. "I'll return later. I'd better go check on my sister."

"Nah, don't worry about comin' back. Going home. Pa needs help with the horses. He's not been feeling good lately. Not sure what's wrong. Doc's been out a few times already." Matthew's solemn expression took Mitch by surprise. His boyhood friend gulped down his drink. "I won't be spending much time in town anymore. I'm needed at home."

Mitch took him in wondering what his friend wasn't telling him. "I'm sorry to hear about your Pa."

They walked out together. Matthew mounted his horse and headed out of town and Mitch walked toward the schoolhouse, only to stop when spotting Olivia inside his parents' mercantile.

He'd already been there all morning unloading the latest shipment and lining the shelves with new items while at the same time balancing on his ladder and handing objects to patrons who'd gotten wind of the latest arrivals. If he entered, his parents would put him to work and he didn't plan to spend the rest of the day inside the busy store. Instead, he loitered on the side of the building waiting for Olivia to exit.

Parcels stacked high in her arms, Olivia didn't see him right away. She sidestepped a small dog that scampered by with a prize of a meaty bone and her parcels began to slide sideways. Mitch caught her packages and lifted most of them away to wide eyes meeting his.

"Oh! Mitch, I didn't expect to see you." She eyed the bundles in his hands. "Thank you. I should have made two trips." Olivia did not smile. "My buggy is over here." She put her parcels on the floorboards and reached for the ones he held. Mitch ignored her outstretched hands and placed them beside the ones she'd stowed.

He straightened and looked to her. "How are you, Olivia?"

"I'm well. Thank you for helping me."

He took her elbow and steered her to stand under the building's porch. "I'm sorry about the other day. I overreacted."

"Yes, you did," she replied. "I don't know what you were thinking."

"I wasn't," Mitch replied. He fought the urge to reach for her, once more to feel her soft curves against him when he held her. They'd kissed several times on their outings and he missed her. They'd spent hours talking about everything and nothing. For the first time in his life, he was able to relax with a woman. She never pushed him for a commitment.

He peered into her veiled eyes. "I miss spending time with you."

Olivia inhaled and looked away. "It's best we don't continue whatever this is." She waved her hand back and forth between them. "I want a husband and children, a family. You've made it perfectly clear you don't. My parents are pushing for Matthew Corson to court me."

At the sound of his friend's name, Mitch huffed sharply. Was that why Matthew acted differently earlier? "Have you talked with Matthew about it?"

"Not yet, no," Olivia pressed her lips together and frowned. "His father is sick and wants Matthew to take over the ranch and all. Anyhow, Misses Corson told my mother he is looking to settle down and so they want us to spend time together. I am not against it, Mitch." Resigned eyes swept his face. "Is there any reason for me not to marry Matthew?"

Mitch could barely swallow past the lump that lodged in his throat. Not trusting himself to speak, he could only stare at his boots and shake his head.

"Good bye, Mitch."

When he looked up, she'd gone.

Chapter Ten

The clanks of forks on plates were the only sounds in the dining room. Nora, Mitch and their mother ate in silence, each lost in their musings. It suited Nora just fine. After leaving the schoolhouse, she'd gone to the mercantile to help her parents. Outside the saloon, she'd spotted Grayson with a saloon girl. He stood outside with the woman, deep in conversation. If that didn't speak volumes of his disregard for her, nothing did. He'd gone straight to a saloon girl after spending the night at her house. Not only that, but he'd called her by his wife's name. "Sophia." Clearly she'd heard him murmur the name between kisses. He did not seem to even realize it. Nora blinked back angry tears and gripped her fork pushing the now cold food around her plate.

"We're ending your engagement," her mother said, pulling Nora away from her thoughts. "Your father has gone to the Cole ranch to speak to Hank. As much as I'd like to see you married, we are not about to allow you to marry into the family of a killer."

"Ashley didn't kill that man," Nora replied. No matter how hurt she was by Grayson's actions, she believed him when it came to his brother being innocent.

"Oh, Nora, you're such a kind-hearted person." Her

mother shook her head. "There is something wrong with that boy. He's not been the same since he came back from wherever he went with the cavalry."

Carolyn continued her explanation. "Anyway, as I was saying, your father will be speaking to Hank Cole and will let him know that the engagement is off. I know they'll understand that it should be handled discreetly. We'll just say you couldn't abide Grayson Cole's behavior. Why that boy was chasing after Olivia Dougherty, knowing full well she's your brother's girl, I'll never know."

At hearing Olivia's name, Mitch straightened. "She's not my girl. Not anymore." He pushed away from the table. "Ma, you need to let us live our lives and make our own decisions. Nora didn't want to get married in the first place. Your pushing this engagement is what got her in this mess to begin with. What is wrong with us choosing who and when we marry?" He picked up his hat from a nearby chair and stormed from the house.

Carolyn Banks placed her palm over her chest. "What in the world's gotten into that boy?" She dropped her arm. "Besides, Grayson has the most horrible reputation. Why, it was just a few weeks ago that he rode out of town half naked after jumping out of Mary Morrison's window. Her husband came home early from a cattle drive. That boy's lucky Jay Morrison is too gullible to figure things out and shoot him."

Nora did not reply. She stood and picked up the dinner plates. "I'll clean up, Mother. Why don't you put your feet up? You know how they swell from standing all day at the store."

It was easy to dissuade her mother from cleaning up. She flashed Nora a grateful smile and shuffled out of the room.

A heavy weight lodged into Nora's chest. Instead of relief at the opportunity that presented itself to easily end the engagement with Grayson, annoyance filled her. That they could not make a decision on their own didn't sit well with her. Tomorrow, she'd seek out Grayson and speak to him. Although he'd probably be glad to be rid of her and the situation, she needed to speak to him and personally ensure he knew she was unaware of her father's visit to his family. Grayson's actions the night before contradicted every rumor she'd heard about him. He'd not pressed her to take things forward. Just as he'd promised, he remained in the front room, bundled in blankets fast asleep when she'd slipped out that morning. Why did her foolish heart pick him and not Bronson?

The warm dishwater soothed her skin and the picture of Grayson's heated kisses, the warmth of his large body against hers, entered her mind. Her lips curved at remembering how his long hair fell forward, the silken tresses swinging back and forth when he leaned over her. With a deep sigh, she closed her eyes. At least no one could take her memory of the special moments she shared with him.

Nora spent the next day at Banks' Mercantile, after cancelling classes for the week. There was no use in holding school for the three children who'd show up. The rest of her students were all staying home to help with spring planting. Perched on a ladder, she dusted a long shelf and lifted jars from the lower one up to the higher shelf arranging them in straight lines. Satisfied with the organized items, she climbed down to gather more cleaning cloths from the back room.

"How about some of that jerky? I'd like a dollar's worth." *That voice.* The gruff male voice shot like ice down her veins and Nora froze, not daring to turn around. The timbre was exactly as she remembered it against her ear, that dark night. Her heart hammered so hard she feared it would break free from her chest and her mouth dried, making it impossible to swallow.

No, Nora didn't have to look to know it was him, the last person she ever thought to see again. The one man she wished never to cross paths with.

From her peripheral vision, she saw her mother smile as she chatted good-naturedly while weighing the items. "It's quite good. We get it from a family on the outskirts of town. They refuse to share the recipe...."

Nora dared a look over her left shoulder, away from the man and her mother. Her father was unloading some fabric onto a large bin while at the same time helping another customer and her husband. Once assured her parents were safe, she dropped the soiled cloths and dashed out the back door. It was imperative to keep Mitch from entering while that man was there.

Nora practically ran into her brother. Mitch carried a case full of jars towards the back entry. Heart pounding, she struggled to get words past her parched throat

"Hold the door open," Mitch demanded while he grunted under the weight of his burden.

Nora blocked his path and allowed the door to close. "I'm going to be sick, Mitch," Nora croaked and grabbed for his arm wrapping her hand around it.

"Stop now, you're going to make me drop this case of molasses. It's heavy." Mitch wobbled but managed to keep the crate upright.

"Please, don't go inside, not right now." Nora knew that if Mitch entered the building he'd not hesitate to kill the man, not caring who witnessed it. Her secret would be out and Mitch would hang for murder.

"You're white as a ghost," Mitch told her, concern etched across his handsome face. "Are you about to pass out?"

With narrowed eyes, her brother looked to the back wall of the building. "Why? Who's in there?" Nora was glad when he placed his burden down and came to her and took her by the shoulders to guide her to sit on a crate.

What if the man was inside with intent to steal? Holding her parents at gunpoint while she fought to keep Mitch outside. God.

"Nora?"

Focusing on his face, she realized her mind had wandered and she forced her breathing to slow. Unfortunately, her mind went back to what was happening inside.

"I'm going to get Ma. You don't seem well at all." Mitch went to stand, but Nora grabbed his arm, her mind scrambling, trying to come up with something to tell her brother.

"Mitch, you should marry Olivia, settle down, start a family. I know you care for her and she for you," she blurted. "Go talk to her, tell her how you feel. I want the best for you and it breaks my heart to know how often you're over at that saloon."

Mitch frowned at her words, but her tactic worked. His attention was redirected from her pallor. "What do I have to offer?" Her brother's shoulders fell forward. "I don't own a damn thing, not land, not a house, nothing. I sleep above the mercantile for goodness sakes."

"That can be fixed easily enough. You've saved enough money that you can buy some land and build a house." Nora reached forward and placed a hand on his jaw. "Why do you not marry, Mitch? Tell me the truth. Is it because of me?"

"No...of course not." Mitch's hesitant reply did not convince her. Tormented eyes met hers and his words broke her heart. "If I could not save you, how can I expect to keep a wife from harm? Be the protector of a family?"

The knowledge of how much that man had taken from both of them turned her vision red. Nora stomped her foot. "For God's sakes, Mitch! You were sixteen, barely a man. Of course that bastard overtook you. It was him in the wrong about everything. Not us! We were only kids." She huffed and lowered her voice. "Besides, things are different now. You are tall and quite strong. Not to mention a great shot. It would never happen now."

A smile curved Mitch's lips. "Thanks, sis. But Olivia is not the woman for me. She wants more than I have, more than who I am. I do care for her, but not in the way a man cares for the woman he wishes to marry." He stood and picked up the crate again. "Now, please open the door for me."

Dread rose up her body with each step she took behind her brother into the mercantile. She strained to listen for the raspy tone. Someone spoke. It was a male voice, but it didn't sound like the man. Instead, it was the familiar deep timbre of Grayson's voice. A different type of apprehension took hold. Were both Grayson and the man here?

Mitch moved aside and the entire space came into view. An elderly lady with a basket hanging from her arm picked through a bushel of apples. The only other person in the mercantile, besides her parents, was Grayson. Strong, broad shoulders bunched as he took the bundle her mother proffered and, at the same time, his blue eyes met hers. His lips lifted into a lazy smile. "Hello, Nora." Her stomach pitched, her entire body tingling and coming to life as she attempted to smile in return.

Her father cleared his throat and her mother glared at him. Before her parents could speak, Nora rushed to Grayson and took his arm. "Let's step outside. I must speak with you."

"All right," Grayson replied and glanced over to Mitch. "Everything good between us?"

Mitch nodded wordlessly, his eyes locked on where she held on to Grayson's arm. "I apologize. I overreacted. Not sure what I was thinkin'."

Seeming to be satisfied with Mitch's answer, Grayson allowed her to pull him toward the door and outside to stand by the hitching posts. "Something's wrong, isn't it?" Brows drawn, he looked down at her. "What happened?"

"You haven't been home yet?" Nora asked.

"Not until I have a clear answer about what's going to happen with my brother. Why? Did something happen at Cole ranch?" He looked toward the stables where she assumed his horse was.

"Nothing is wrong at your home, Grayson. Although, with Ashley in jail, complications have arisen between our families."

He interrupted. "I can speak to your parents. I talked to Lizzie earlier, one of the saloon girls. She told me the night Walters was killed he had an argument over a game of cards with a grey-bearded stranger. I have to find that man. My gut tells me he's the killer."

Guilt assailed her. Grayson was actually telling her why he'd been talking to the saloon girl. The man before her was so unaware of how his speaking to the saloon girl came across that he actually seemed at ease telling her about it. He didn't suspect she'd find his conversation with the girl in bad taste or an affront to her. Nora met his earnest eyes and took a breath. "I believe I know who that stranger is. I may also know where he's staying."

"How?"

"It doesn't matter how I know, but I do." She looked over her shoulder to ensure Mitch did not come out. "I need you to promise me that my brother won't know anything about this. You can speak to the sheriff, get some men together."

Although he frowned in the direction of the doorway, Grayson did not question her about motives. He nodded. "Dawson isn't much help right now. I'll get Bronson and we'll capture him ourselves."

"There's something else," Nora told him, suddenly feeling exhausted. "My father went to see yours and broke our engagement because of the situation with Ashley. I suppose it makes it easier for us."

Grayson's eyes widened and his lips parted. He reached for his hat and yanked it off his head slapping it on his leg. "Shouldn't that decision be up to us? What is this, the sixteen hundreds where marriages are arranged by parents?"

In spite of the situation, Nora couldn't help a sad smile. "I thought you'd be happy to hear that you're free of this. Of me."

"I suppose it's better than we planned."

She inhaled sharply, his words cutting into her chest, but she ignored the sting, pushed it away. Grayson watched her closely. "Is it what you want, Nora? To be free of me?" The questions took her by surprise, as did the intensity of his stare. "I mean, after what happened between us...I'm not so sure about wanting to break off our engagement. What I'm saying is...well, I think we should take a day or so and then decide."

"I'm confused. You have been so adamant about not wanting to ever settle down," Nora told him, not looking away. "Why do you need to think about it?"

"Because," he leaned forward and pressed his lips to hers, "I can't stop thinking about you. I'm not ready to let you go." He then turned and departed, leaving her confused.

Minutes after he walked away, Nora remained in front of the building, her mind awhirl. *Not ready to let you go.* The unexpected words lifted her spirits from the bare bottom they'd hit upon the stranger reentering her life.

Then she realized he said he wasn't ready to let her go. It did not mean he planned to marry her. Her soul sank. She wasn't strong enough to go through that heartbreak.

Not that her heart wasn't already going through a lashing.

Chapter Eleven

The cold chill of premonition shook him and Ashley jerked up to sit. Something was wrong. One of his brothers was in danger. It had to be Grayson. It was always Grayson getting into scrapes, needing him. What was the boy up to this time?

"Deputy?" he called out, his voice hoarse from lack of use.

"What do you want?" the man yelled from the front office.

"Let me out now," he growled.

"Right. That's the last thing you can expect, Cole."

"I mean it, Deputy, if you don't let me out, something bad is going to happen. I need to get out of here."

"Why don't you try and get past the cell door and do just that," the deputy called back with a mirthless chuckle. "Idiot."

Just then, the sound of footsteps grabbed Ashley's attention. Sheriff Dawson's voice was low and angry. "That damn Grayson is collecting up a posse. They rode out just minutes ago. From what I hear, they're headed towards Clark River. I need you to come along with me and stop this nonsense."

"Hey!" Ashley yelled. "What about me?"

"You'll be fine. I've got someone coming," Dawson called back. "Don't cause any more problems either. And Ashley, looks like your brother will be sharing the cell with you by nightfall."

More steps sounded, the door slammed and then silence.

Scant minutes later, the door opened and new, softer footfalls crossed the front room. Whoever entered stepped lighter than a man and he wondered who it was. "Hello?"

Silence. Whoever it was did not reply. A chair squeaked as if the person sat, then it was quiet again. Part of him wanted to ignore whoever it was, but it warred against the other half that needed to leave the place and ensure his brother was not about to get himself killed. "Deputy? I'm about to be sick."

No reply came.

"Whoever you are, can you help me?" he forced his voice to sound weak. Thanks to the lack of use, he didn't have to fake the hoarseness. "I need some water. Please."

A huff sounded followed by water being poured. He kept his eyes downcast as the person moved closer. Boots and brown britches neared, the keys to the cells jingled from a belt worn low on a slender waist. Closer and closer still, the new jail keeper moved with caution. Ashley bided his time, waiting for the perfect moment. He coughed and groaned.

A tin cup was proffered between the bars. The arm stretched into the cell and Ashley uncoiled slowly, giving the illusion of having difficulty moving. He reached for the cup and grabbed the man's arm, yanking him roughly against the bars while, with his other hand, he wrapped fingers around his waist and unfastened the key ring.

"Awwww!" The scream startled him so that he almost dropped the keys, but he managed to move past the shock of a female voice. Not releasing her arm, Ashley met the darkest eyes he'd ever seen. Deeper than the night sky, so dark he could not make out the pupils. The woman groaned in pain and he released his hold just enough so as not to hurt her more.

"Don't move," he grunted and took her face in. Heart-shaped with a rosebud for a mouth, she looked more like an angel than a tomboy. The midnight black tresses that were not collected back into a braid of sorts were tussled about her beautiful face, framing it perfectly.

The woman grimaced when Ashley maneuvered around to slip the key into the lock. "Damn it, Ashley. Pa's gonna kill me! Why the hell can't you just stay in there? He's gonna get you anyway."

"How do you know me?" He couldn't help but gape at her when she bit her bottom lip and released the now moistened pink pout.

"Doesn't matter," she snapped and attempted to wiggle her arm free. "You're hurting me."

The clink of the lock releasing followed by the squeak of the cell door opening seemed to anger her further. "Now look here, Ashley Cole. Don't think I'm not going to chase after you and get you right back in there."

They shuffled, her walking backward along with the door, each of them on opposite sides, as he held her by her arm against the bars. Ashley released her arm and rushed around the door. As he expected, she ran for the front office and whatever firearm her father left for her to use. Either that or she was running out the front door to yell for help.

She chose the rifle, but before she could reach it, Ashley grabbed her from behind and they tumbled onto the floor. The wildcat scratched, kicked and bit at him.

"Umph!" Stars sprang up behind his eyelids when her knee connected between his legs. Ashley did not release her. Instead, he rolled with her so that he lay over her allowing his weight to assist in holding her still until he recovered enough to breathe normally. He panted against the side of her face, keeping his head turned while making it impossible for her to move.

She growled and attempted to bite at his face, but

Ashley lifted out of her reach. "Stop now! Hold still. I don't want to hurt you."

"I want to hurt you. Get off me," she replied and attempted to buck him off. Small as she was, the movement barely registered. Despite the now dull ache, his body responded to the female under him.

Ashley stretched her arms up over her head and let out a breath. "I'm going to release you and walk out of here. Don't you dare shoot me in the butt for doing this, you understand?"

Her eyes met his and for a moment the only sound in the room was their heavy breathing. Then something unexpected happened. Her eyes slid to his mouth.

The woman caught herself and jerked her face to the side, which only affected Ashley more as the slender expanse of her neck led his gaze to travel to her chest, which heaved up and down with every breath. Two buttons had popped off and he could see the swell of her breasts, the creamy skin begging for his touch.

Ashley cleared his throat. He had to get off her and fast. "Answer me."

"Fine. Yeah." She rolled to her side when he lifted off of her just enough so she could breathe easier. "Let me go."

He rose, grabbed the rifle and moved to stand between the woman and the doorway. Her eyes locked on to the weapon, but she did not show any signs of fear. Quite the opposite, her right eyebrow rose in a challenging manner. "What are you going to do with that?"

"I'm going after my brother to make sure he doesn't get hurt. I'll return it afterwards. And I'll come back to be locked up if it's still required."

She frowned but said nothing. Her left hand lifted to her right upper arm and she began to massage the skin where he'd grabbed her.

"I'm sorry if I hurt you," Ashley told her, meaning it, and backed toward the doorway. "I have to get to my brother."

"It's a stupid thing to do." Her eyes narrowed and she went to sit at the desk. "But suit yourself."

Ashley turned and walked out.

Grayson and three men he convinced to come along to search for the stranger rode hard for two hours to the general location Nora directed him to. The path, once connecting Alder Gulch and Virginia City, had become overgrown from lack of use, but they managed to keep the horses on the trail. Since the railroad had come in, most people used the lower roads closer to the tracks, which made this a perfect place for someone to hide. He hoped Nora was correct and there was a cabin nearby, otherwise, he was wasting an entire day for nothing. It bothered him that Nora knew this stranger. He would ask later how she was acquainted with this man and where he hid.

"There," one of the men motioned with his hand. "I see something."

Guiding the horses around the perimeter of the clearing where a lone shack of a house stood, the men kept quiet using only hand signals to communicate. Once they got to a distance where the sounds from the horses could give them away, they dismounted and walked.

The lone, dilapidated hovel appeared empty, but the evidence of recently chopped wood told of a recent visitor.

Branches crunched under his boots with every step as Grayson moved from his horse to take shelter behind a tree to get a better look at the dwelling. The sounds of hooves made them all turn to see Sheriff Dawson and his deputy arrive. Grayson swore under his breath. Of course the man would try to stop them. He'd be damned if he'd allow it.

Without waiting for the sheriff to get any closer, he bent low and ran to the seemingly empty shack.

Grayson peered through the grimy windows and saw evidence that, indeed, someone was using the place and recently by the looks of it. A plate and cup were on the lopsided table as well as a dirty coffee pot on the wood-burning stove. He peered at the rumpled bedroll. No one was inside.

"Cole, don't you go in. None of you move," Dawson called out. Good thing it was empty, otherwise the sheriff would have given whoever was inside plenty of notice. Grayson continued to the front door and dashed inside.

The sheriff materialized on his heels, but no one else moved. Obviously, the other men had taken heed and remained outside with the deputy who stood a safe distance away. "Dammit, Grayson, what the hell are you doing?"

"What you're not," Grayson replied rifling through a rucksack he discovered. He pulled out a money clip with a big "W" engraved in it as well as a watch. "Bet if you check, these things belonged to Walters." He threw them onto the table and stalked from the place.

Another horseman neared and everyone pulled their guns, holding them at a ready. Grayson squinted and let another ripe curse out. "Put your guns down. It's my brother."

The sheriff walked outside pointing his gun at Ashley. "I'm not so sure I shouldn't shoot him for escaping from jail."

"The hell you will." Grayson held the muzzle of his gun to the man's temple, not flinching at the click of another weapon at his own, held by the deputy.

Ashley raced closer, his horse heaving hard breaths and prancing when he pulled it to a stop. His keen eyes locked on to the sheriff. "I'll go back to jail. I'm just making sure my brother didn't come to harm."

The sheriff did not lower his weapon. His gaze slid to

Grayson, who continued to hold his gun up. "Both of you will be locked up if this doesn't clear you," he gritted out. "Where's Grace?"

Brows drawn, Ashley gave the sheriff a one-shouldered shrug. "If you're referring to your newest deputy, last I saw her she was sitting at the desk. Mad as all get out, but unharmed."

Finally, the lawman lowered his weapon and the other two lowered as well. "There better not be one bruise on her." He looked to Grayson. "Even if these articles prove to be Walters', it doesn't prove Ashley's innocence. A judge will have to decide."

The sheriff stalked to his horse and mounted, followed by his deputy. Ashley remained mounted, his eyes sliding over Grayson as if to ensure he were unharmed. Grayson cleared his throat. "Is my brother to remain your prisoner?"

Annoyance etched across Dawson's features as he regarded Ashley. "I suppose you'll stick around if I let you go. But be warned, if I find you're the one who's been hiding out here, I'm coming back for you."

"Wait," Ashley moved closer to the sheriff, whose entire body tensed. Ashley held out the rifle he'd stowed on the saddle holder. "It's yours." It disappeared from his hand and the sheriff huffed and shoved it into his own holder. "See that you stay around these parts, Ashley." With one last glare at Grayson, the lawman guided his steed away and kicked it into a gallop. The rest of the men followed suit, several of them shaking their heads and finally allowing smiles loose at the sheriff's retreating form.

With purposeful strides, Grayson went to his horse and mounted. He drew up next to his brother. "Should we find a comfortable place to camp? The stranger, whoever he is, hasn't left. All his things are still in there." He motioned toward the shack with his head. "Maybe he isn't aware we came here and will come to see about his belongings before leaving."

Ashley frowned and scanned the area. "It's hard to tell. With so many horses and all the ruckus, if he was near, he's clean gone by now."

The brothers settled soon after in a clearing not too far from the stranger's hiding place. Grayson looked to Ashley. "Thank you."

Ashley grunted and chewed on some jerky. "It's what brothers do. Besides, you did all this because of me."

Chapter Twelve

Nora settled into her steamy bath and sighed. Finally, relaxation after a day of flinching every time the door to the mercantile opened. In the quiet of the moment, her mind wandered to Grayson. Had he found the stranger? If so, what had occurred?

Gossip from two women that entered the mercantile informed her that Ashley was no longer in jail and that the sheriff was enraged at his daughter, Grace, for allowing him to escape.

She tried to picture Grace Dawson. The young woman had always been on the fringes of her friendship circles, preferring ranching to sewing and teas. Much to her mother's chagrin, the sheriff encouraged the girl's wild ways. Although Nora had spent time with her years ago when attending Sunday school, Grace was older now. Maybe she'd grown to be more feminine.

When someone rapped on the front door, she gasped and realized she'd been in the water so long it had cooled considerably. Nora didn't expect anyone. For goodness sakes, it was almost seven in the evening. The only person who visited so late, on occasion, was her brother. Reaching for a towel, she climbed from the tub and dried before wrapping a robe around her body.

Trembling from the cool air, she tiptoed to the window and peeked out through the curtains. A dark figure stood at her doorstep, the face hidden by shadows. But she could tell it was a male by the size of the figure.

"Nora? It's Sheriff Dawson."

Relief left her in waves as she went to the doorway. She cracked it just enough to peek out. "I'm sorry, Sheriff Dawson, I'm not dressed. What can I do for you?"

The man looked away, his face reddening. "I do apologize for the lateness, but I must ask you some questions. I can wait out here until you dress."

She nodded and looked past him to the street. The last things she needed were the town gossips wondering why the sheriff visited and the news getting to Mitch. "Please come in, I'll be right back." After opening the door, she dashed to her bedroom to change.

Nora poured hot coffee into a cup and continued in her attempt to make up a story as to why she was aware of where the stranger lived. "So as you see, the other day, after the stranger came to the mercantile, I happened to be out riding and caught sight of the man going toward the abandoned cabin over by the lake. I mentioned it to Grayson Cole when he came to the store a day later and told me he'd heard about an argument between Walters and a stranger."

"Why would Cole confide this information to you?" Sheriff Dawson frowned while waiting for her reply.

"We were, er...are...engaged."

His brows rose and he blinked several times before formulating some sort of reply. "I wasn't aware."

Nora took a breath. "Is there anything else, Sheriff?"

Dawson studied her for a moment. "I wonder if you would assist in any way to free your future brother-in-law."

Since it was not a question, Nora remained quiet while she pictured kicking the irritating man under the table.

Sheriff Dawson was not a bad person. If anything, he was an excellent lawman. But this questioning could have waited for a more sensible hour to say the least.

Relief filled her when he reached for his hat and stood. "Again, I apologize for coming so late. It's just that wondering how you knew where that man hid would have bothered me all night. Thank you for your time, Miss Banks."

She followed him to the door and waited patiently until the man descended the stairs from her porch before she closed it behind him and sagged against the door. If only she knew where the stranger was, it would be easier to keep from running into him. Or worse, that Mitch happened upon him.

"Nora?" Mitch knocked on her bedroom door. "Are you all right?"

She bolted upright and noticed that the room was alight with sunshine. "Oh lord, how late is it?" she mumbled, scrambling from the bed, grabbing her robe and wrapping it tightly around her just as Mitch walked in.

His eyes assessed her and a smile curved his lips. "You sleeping in today, sister? Ma sent me to check on you when you didn't show up at eleven. I used my key to come in when you didn't answer my knocking."

"What?" she searched around until seeing the small clock on her dresser. "Goodness, I've never slept this late."

"You deserve the rest. You probably need it, especially after how unwell you looked yesterday. Why don't you spend the day at home?"

An idea came to her and she nodded to her brother. "Good idea. I will take a day of leisure. As a matter of fact, I may just go for a ride. Get some fresh air."

"I can go with you when I finish unloading. It won't take me long." Of course, her brother, always protective, would insist. Nora could kick herself for blurting out the idea.

"Well, I'm not sure yet. If I do, I will come fetch you." She gave him what, hopefully, came across as a bright smile. "I better get dressed and make some tea. Care for some?"

He shook his head and moved toward the door and stopped abruptly. "Why are there two coffee cups on the table? Who was here?"

Frozen on the spot, Nora looked to the table as if to confirm what he stated. "I—I suppose I've been getting messy. No one has been here, both are mine."

Mitch was already heading outside and she breathed a sigh of relief with only a tingle of guilt. Her brother trusted her. He never expected her to keep any secrets from him. And she'd never lied to him before, but in this, it was imperative he not find out who was in town.

After dressing in a simple, faded calico shirt and a serviceable riding skirt, she pulled her long, wavy hair into the familiar hairstyle of a loose bun at her nape. She placed her hat low toward the front of her face and left to where her horse was stabled.

The sheriff hadn't arrested the stranger, so he was still on the loose. Her mind was made up. She'd kill him before allowing harm to come to Mitch or her.

Riding astride, Nora made good time to the one area she'd avoided for many years. The grass was tall and green from the recent rains and wild flowers bloomed, adding sprinkles of blue and yellow. With a loud squawk, a falcon flew overhead and she followed its decent into the tree line noting how dense the forest had become.

Once she left the pathway, she slowed, keeping a keen ear for any noise. From her vantage point atop the horse, Nora didn't have to go too close to get a good view of the shack.

Looking to the right and left, she found a place where she'd tether the horse and she guided her steed there. With swift moves, she dismounted and tied the horse to a low branch. Her vision blurred and she held her hand up to the tree. God, she needed to keep it together, no matter how terrifying the situation, there was no other way. This man had taken so much from them already. She would not allow him to take anything more. Nora pushed past the panic that threatened to choke her and inhaled deeply.

Unaccustomed to the weight of a gun belt at her hips, Nora pulled at it with shaking hands and arranged the leather.

She pulled the revolver from the belt and turned toward the shack only to gasp when a hand covered her mouth and an arm coiled around her center.

Terror squeezed in her chest and made it impossible to breathe. She was dragged backward a few feet before she remembered she had a gun. Waiting for the perfect moment, Nora allowed the man to continue to drag her until he finally stopped and spoke. "What in the hell are you doing here, Nora?"

It was Grayson. Tears of relief stung and she blinked them away only to notice he stared at the gun in her hand.

Determined not to show weakness, Nora looked him straight in the eye. "There is something I have to do. To protect Mitch." Chin jutted forward, she held her head high. "You'd do the same for your brother in my place."

"He has." Ashley stepped out behind Grayson.

"I don't know why you think your brother needs protecting, but you have to leave." Grayson neared and took her by the shoulders. "This is too dangerous. We are waiting for the stranger and we're going to take him in if he's not spooked by now with so many people coming and going." Brilliant blue eyes bore into hers. "Please."

"At this point, it's more dangerous for her to return alone," Ashley chimed in, his deep voice flat.

Grayson sighed and looked towards the shack. "I think it's a lost cause anyway. He didn't show last night. I think he's on to us, probably long gone. Why are you so adamant about this man, Nora?" He dropped his hands from her shoulders and Nora could not think of what to say, not to him. Never would she admit her shame.

Taking two steps back, she turned toward the house and holstered her gun. "He's not there?" her voice barely above a whisper.

"Nope, I think we need to head back to town," Grayson replied, coming up behind her. "Do you know this man?"

An involuntary shudder shook her. "In a way, yes."

"You planned to kill him, didn't you?"

"Yes, I did," Nora told him, her eyes meeting his. "I want him dead."

It struck her as strange that Grayson did not react. He looked toward the shack, instead. "Let's go, Nora. I'll escort you home."

Perhaps the stranger was gone and nothing would come of it. For a few more seconds, she stared at the house. Hopefully, all the comings and goings did spook him into leaving town. Unfortunately, the heaviness in her stomach warned her that something bad was about to happen.

"Are you all right?" Grayson took her arm and turned her to face him. "You've turned pale. Talk to me."

The earnest depth of his expression almost brought the story out of her, but she bit down against it. "It's nothing more than fatigue." Without meaning to, she glanced back toward the shack. "I sure hope he's gone."

"Come on." Grayson led her to where her horse was tethered and gave her a leg up to mount. Once she did, he motioned for her to remain. "Let me get my horse. I'll be right back."

Grayson dashed into the trees.

His watchful gaze on his brother's retreating form, Ashley moved to stand next to her. Both remained quiet waiting for Grayson.

A loud pop sounded, echoing through the woods. Dread slammed into Nora and she jerked toward Ashley who sprinted in the direction Grayson had gone.

Chapter Thirteen

"Are you sure you found Nora to be well?" his mother asked for the third time, her eyes going from Mitch to the door. "It's not like her to stay all day in bed."

Mitch reached behind the counter to find a cloth and wiped the sweat from his face. He eyed the large bags of rice he'd just carried in and nodded. "Yes, Ma, she was just tired. Said she planned to rest today. Also said if she decided to go out for fresh air, she'd come by and fetch me to go with her."

A woman neared and glanced at him. Obviously, she'd been listening in on their conversation. "I just saw Nora heading out of town on horseback. Riding astride, no less." She lifted her nose in distaste. "In my day, women would never be caught riding, much less astride."

His mother neared and patted Mitch's arm. "She must be feeling better. She should have come by and assured me. With me being so worried about your father, all this is making me overly anxious." She made a sweeping motion with her hand across the store. "I'll need you here all day. With the new shipment, people are already spreading the word. My hip has been bothering me, so I can't stand all day..."

She continued prattling and Mitch was forced to wait for her to take a breath. "Ma, what's wrong with Pa?"

"Oh!" Carolyn's high-pitched exclamation made several customers turn to her. She waved away any concern, which created more curiosity. Leave it to his mother to make everything about her. "He's been up all night, something about chest pains. I told him he ate too much of that rich stew last night."

"How was he this morning?" Mitch's pulse quickened. "Ma, have you checked on him today?" Not waiting for an answer he spun and raced to the back of the building.

"Mitch, don't you be gone too long," his mother called after him.

His mother would have to make do.

The time it took him to run the two blocks to his house seemed like an eternity, but Mitch finally arrived and burst through the door. "Pa?" He rushed through the kitchen and family room to find them empty. "Pa!" Mitch called out again into the eerily silent home. Heart hammering beneath his chest, he raced up the stairs to his parents' bedroom.

His father lay slumped over, half off the large bed, his coloring absolutely pasty white. Mitch grabbed his arms and pulled him onto the bed before reaching with a shaky hand to the man's throat. "Pa?" he whispered and felt for a pulse.

The beat under his fingers was ever so slight. Mitch wondered if he'd willed it. "Hang on, Pa. I'm going to fetch Doc Dougherty." He pulled the covers over his pale father and sprinted out the front doorway.

Breath rasped in and out of his mouth when Mitch arrived at the doctor's office another two blocks away. Without preamble, he walked past the empty front area into the back room.

A woman lying on the table gasped and yanked a sheet over herself. Both Olivia and the doctor turned to him with eyebrows high at his trespass. "Mitch Banks, get out of here immediately," Doctor Dougherty snapped. "What in the heck do you mean by bursting in here like this."

"I'm sorry," Mitch said to the woman turning his back. "Doc, you gotta come now. I think my pa is dying."

"Father, get your bag. I'll stay with Missus Johnson and help her get dressed," Olivia told her father. "Come to the front office please." Olivia took Mitch's arm and led him to the anterior room.

Once in the front office, Mitch began to shake, his eyes jerking from Olivia to the back room. "He has to hurry." In spite of the dire circumstances, he wanted nothing more at the moment than to collapse onto the floor, for it all to be a strange dream that he'd wake from.

"Come on," the doctor's gruff voice pulled him back to the reality that his father could be dying and his sister had gone off somewhere without his protection.

He moved away from Olivia and followed the doctor who stalked out without glancing back to ensure Mitch followed.

They made their way to the house with Mitch arriving before the doctor. His father seemed to be the same, his breathing barely noticeable.

The physician entered the bedroom. He asked Mitch to wait outside while he examined Arthur Banks.

At his parents' front doorway, Mitch scanned the street hoping to spot Nora. Life went on as usual in the town, it seemed. People moved about taking care of whatever daily business was needed. Finally, he heard footsteps and jerked around at hearing his name.

Doctor Dougherty looked up as Mitch walked into the darkened room. His father remained still, paler, if that was possible. The sunken, closed eyes did not trouble him as much as the lack of his chest rising with breathing. "Is he all right, Doc?"

"I'm sorry, son. He just died."

"I should have stayed with him," Mitch told the doctor, his eyes locked to his father's face. "What happened to him?"

The doctor pulled the sheet over the dead man's face.

"Heart attack. There was nothing that could be done." Doctor Dougherty stood. "I would like to accompany you to speak with your mother."

Unable to pull his eyes from the sheet-covered figure that he'd shared dinner with the night before, Mitch could only nod. A haze surrounded him and he closed the distance between the doctor and the bed. "Are you sure doctor? He is dead?"

Kindness filled the doctor's eyes and Mitch swung away not wanting to see it, not now when he was so close to losing the ability to maintain his composure. He had to stay strong for his mother, who would be devastated. Their father doted upon her, taking care of every little nuance that she came up with. How would she handle the news? What about Nora?

As if separate from his body, his feet moved him behind the doctor and down the stairs to the front door. He wasn't sure how long it took to get to the store, but when they entered the mercantile, he was surprised they'd arrived. The doctor moved toward the counter where Carolyn Banks had just finished handing a bundle to a customer. She directed an angry glare to Mitch, but then smiled at Doctor Dougherty. "How are you Calvin? What can I get for you?"

The click of the lock on the door seemed to echo through the space when Mitch slid the lock into place after closing the doors.

"Oh God, no!" his mother cried out. He turned just as his mother fell onto the floor in a faint, the doctor barely catching her in time.

Mitch went to the back room and retrieved two blankets; one he rolled and placed under her head and the other covered her still body.

The doctor looked up. "After she's stabilized, I'll help you take her home. Mitch, you have to find Nora before word gets to her."

Chapter Fourteen

Nora dismounted and rushed toward the area where Ashley and Grayson disappeared. There were no sounds or voices coming from the dense brush. Not sure what to do, she moved slowly, her heart pounding hard in her chest, her mouth dry.

"Grayson," she hissed, trying her best to not make too much noise. She avoided stepping on branches, yet something still managed to crunch under her foot. "Ashley?" Branches blocked her way and she pushed them aside to get a better view, but no one was about. Another step forward, then another. Panic seized her and Nora forced back the fear. "Grayson?"

Rustling sounded from her right and she snapped around to look. Nothing came into view. Her heart pounded so hard she doubted the ability to hear much. With a fortifying breath, she continued forward, another two steps.

A twig snapped followed by a cold press of metal to her temple. "Don't move."

It was him. The stranger.

The strangled gasp that sounded from deep in her throat was more animal-like than human. Nora stopped in her tracks, not moving as he ordered. She wouldn't have turned around anyway.. Although she was sure he'd not recognize her, especially after so many years, she never wanted to see his face up close again. Where were Grayson and Ashley? Had he already killed them?

The feeling like that of being dunked in icy water fell over her. She began to shake, her knees threatened to give out.

Everything became eerily silent, not even the sound of a horse or footsteps. The irony that history could repeat itself was not lost on her, but this time she was not a helpless fifteen-year-old girl. This time she'd fight with all her strength.

A hand prodded her back. "Walk slow," the stranger grunted as if the words cost him. "Don't turn around." *No problem with that.*

They walked back the way she had come. All the while, she scanned the area for a possible escape and kept her ears open for any sounds of someone else approaching. Hands to her side, her right one brushed against the butt of her gun. She'd totally forgotten about it. Obviously the folds of her skirts hid the holster, but how long before he noticed the belt at her hips.

Rustling sounded and the man groaned. He yanked her against him with one arm around her shoulders and swung about, holding her in front of him.

Ashley appeared from the brush. Behind him, Grayson stood with his hand on his bleeding midsection. Both men pointed guns at them.

Grayson's eyes roamed over her before he raised them past her head to her captor. Blood seeped from where his hand was placed, but he managed to still appear menacing. "Let her go." His words sounded strong, but she caught the shifting of Ashley's eyes to him. His brother, like her, feared he'd fall over from the injury.

"You're gonna be okay, Nora." Panic filled Grayson's eyes when they met hers and she wondered if it was the injury or if, in actuality, he feared for her. He looked past her to the stranger again. "This has nothing to do with her. Release her now and you can have me."

"I'd say you're not in the position to bargain with me. As a matter of fact, why don't I finish what I started and kill you both."

"No." Nora managed to choke out. "Don't you dare hurt him again."

"Don't say anything else, Nora." Grayson managed to straighten to his full height. Ashley made to move to his brother when the stranger called out to him.

"Don't move." The gun moved from her temple toward the brothers who remained still, each of them staring straight at death without a flinch.

She would not allow the stranger to take more from her. He would not kill the man she loved.

The man fired and Grayson fell back onto the ground. Ashley threw himself over his brother to protect him from being shot again. The stranger pointed at Ashley.

"No!" Nora shoved from him and pulled her gun with one swift motion from its holster. She whirled around and shot the man in the middle of his chest.

His shocked, rounded eyes stared at her, his mouth opened and closed. The only sound was a grunt before he crumpled onto the ground.

Nora stumbled back, the gun still in her hand and covered her mouth with the other. "Oh, God." With dispassionate eyes, she looked down at the man who lay sprawled on the ground. His mouth gulped for air then his head lulled to the side. Nora let out a slow breath. It was over.

Arms wrapped around her and pulled her away from the man. In silence, she allowed Ashley to lead her to where Grayson lay. Ashley then took her gun and placed it back into her holster. "Nora, look at me."

She looked up and the haze lifted.

Ashley placed his hands on her shoulders to keep her attention. "We have to get Grayson to town. He's bleeding something awful." Blue eyes, much darker and somber than Grayson's, searched hers. "Can you help me get him on the horse?"

It was a struggle, but they finally managed to get a sagging Grayson on the horse in front of Ashley. Ashley held Grayson up against his chest. Nora mounted and rode alongside with Grayson's horse tethered to hers. The entire time, her eyes stayed on Grayson whose head flopped forward. Ashley lowered his head every so often and whispered words she could not hear into his ear as they hurried at a steady pace toward town.

Time crawled for Nora. The reality of what happened in the last hour attempted to settle into her mind, but she pushed it away. "Is he breathing?" she asked looking at Ashley who'd once again spoken into Grayson's ear. "We're almost there," she said hoping Grayson could hear her.

"Yes," Ashley replied and kicked the horse into a faster trot. "Hurry."

Once they arrived in town, several men gathered at seeing the wounded Grayson slumped against his brother, blood now running down his pants leg. While they unloaded him, Nora burst into the doctor's office.

Olivia jerked up from where she sat on the desk. Her mouth fell open at seeing Nora and Olivia's hand covered her mouth. "Oh God, Nora, are you hurt? You're covered in blood."

Nora shook her head as the men carried Grayson in. Olivia sprinted into action leading them to the back room and instructing them to lay the injured man on the long table in the center of the space. She eyed Nora once again and then looked to one of the men who'd helped. "Go to the mercantile and fetch my father. He just went there a few moments ago."

Ignoring the rest of the conversations, Nora reached for Grayson's hand and lifted it to her face. She watched his face for a reaction when Olivia cut away his shirt to expose two gunshot wounds, one on his right pectoral and the other one lower on his left side.

"Get me hot water," Olivia instructed Ashley who hurried to do as she bid. The young woman, obviously used to assisting her father, wasted no time. She cleaned away the blood, then took a bundle of clean cloths and put one on the upper chest. "Press down, Nora. Hold it in place. I have to stop the bleeding on this lower one."

After a swift glance to ensure Nora did as instructed, Olivia took a long metal set of prongs, held the flesh of the wound open and dug her fingers into Grayson's side. His moan was soft, but the sound gave Nora some reassurance.

"There it is," Olivia pulled out a bloody bullet and pushed another clean cloth into the wound while she turned to gather other instruments.

Ashley returned with a pot of hot water and placed it where she directed. At the same time, Sheriff Dawson and his daughter arrived.

"Who shot him?" The sheriff neared to peer down at Grayson. He moved back when Olivia motioned with a bloody hand for him to do so.

"The stranger." Ashley did not look to the sheriff. He was too busy concentrating on his brother.

Brows drawn in concentration, Olivia looked to Ashley. "I am going to stitch him up. If he begins to move, hold him in place. I need someone to hand me instruments. Can you wash your hands and help me, Grace?"

The girl rushed to do as she bid, the water from the pitcher splashing into the basin. She then stood next to the tray of instruments and waited further instruction.

It didn't take long for Olivia to complete stitching the wound and then she removed the second bullet in Grayson's chest. She declared it cleared anything vital and began to stitch that wound. All the while, Ashley and Grace helped her, the two of them moving with precision, concentrating on whatever Olivia told them.

Nora remained at Grayson's head. She whispered

words of encouragement into his ear and held his hand. When he'd stopped reacting to the ministrations, fear crept into her.

"He's passed out, that's all," Olivia said, answering Nora's unasked question. "His breathing is steady, don't worry."

"I'll get more clean hot water." Grace took the pot and stepped to the doorway, past her father who remained, watching in silence.

Grace spoke to someone who'd arrived. Nora looked up as Doctor Dougherty, who'd taken his time in coming, entered. The tall man's eyes went from Grayson to Olivia and lastly to Nora. His eyebrows rose and a flicker of concern crossed his face before he looked away from Nora to the patient. "How is he?" He patted his daughter's shoulder.

Olivia listed what all she'd done, without looking up from stitching the wound. "He's pretty lucky, this bullet was lodged in the muscle and the one on his left side cleared any organs. To ensure there's no infection, I cleaned the wounds thoroughly. He should recover without any complications." She bit the string and exchanged a look with her father who nodded and gave his daughter a tired smile.

"You're a fine physician, Olivia."

The doctor turned to Nora. "Can I speak to you in the front room?"

With reluctance, she released Grayson's hand and followed the doctor to the front room. The sheriff walked alongside and touched her arm. "What the hell happened out there?" He put both hands up when the doctor started to interrupt. "Why did that man shoot Grayson? Where is he now?"

"I shot the stranger. He held a gun to my head. He shot Grayson twice and was about to shoot Ashley." Nora lifted her chin. "He was going to kill me, too. I'm sure of it."

The sheriff finally noticed her gun belt and he honed in on it. "Why did you go out there?"

"I was worried about my fiancé," Nora responded without hesitation.

"Sheriff, I must speak to Nora," the doctor said, motioning for her to sit. "Can't you wait to ask questions? Give everyone a moment. They just went through a rough time."

"I will. Just one more thing, Nora," Sheriff Dawson persisted. "Are you sure Ashley didn't shoot him?"

"I shot him Sheriff Dawson! Ashley was caring for Grayson who was already wounded and bleeding!" Nora yelled and began to tremble. "I killed a man today Sheriff Dawson. So just let me be for now, please."

She sank into the chair, thankful when the man went through the doorway.

"Nora, I'm afraid I have more bad news." The doctor lowered to the chair next to hers and peered at her, his eyes kind behind the spectacles. "You have to come to your parents' house with me right now."

"What happened?" Nora couldn't help but look past the doctor towards the back room. She preferred to be there when Grayson woke, to see the bright blue of his eyes when he opened them.

"You father died this morning." Without any inflection in the doctor's voice, she wondered if she heard him right. The words, so flat, yet harsh at the same time, sank into her and the room began to tilt.

When the physician reached for her, she pushed his hands away and stood, which made the room swirl faster. Nora fell against the desk, but pushed away from it. This was not the time for the vapors. Surely the doctor was mistaken. Her father had worked all day yesterday, not once complaining of any ill feeling. Finding steady feet, she went to the front door and out into the waning sunlight.

The familiar combination of furniture varnish and sweet carnations her mother favored and grew struck her first when she entered the darkened interior of her parents' house. Quiet mumblings came from the front parlor and she turned to see several women gathered, including the doctor's wife. Her mother sat in the center of the group wiping a dainty handkerchief below her eyes. She looked up to Nora and then proceeded to take in her appearance and gun belt. Disapproval in her flared nostrils and her hitch of breath struck Nora as inappropriate given the circumstance, yet she neared her mother and kneeled before her. "Is it true?"

"Yes, Nora. Where have you been? What is all over your dress?" Several women gasped and waited for her to reply. Her mother saved her, not one to lose being the center of attention. "Nora, I was alone, with all this happening with only Mitch. Thankfully, Missus Dougherty and Melinda came right away." She pushed a hand against her ample bosom and let out a sob. "What will I ever do without my Arthur?" Nora reached for her mother's hand, but her mother leaned away into a proffered shoulder and began to cry. Her reddened eyes met Nora's. "I am so angry with you right now. Please, just go see about what needs to be done. And for goodness sakes, wash up."

There was only one day that could qualify as worse than this one. Nora sighed and waited, but her mother refused to look at her.

In a way, she was grateful to get away from her mother. She didn't have anything left to give. Besides, the women would take care of her. Right now, she needed to find Mitch. She hurried to her room and removed her holster and gun then headed to her parents' bedroom.

Mitch sat in a chair beside their father's bed. With his forehead resting on his palms, he did not look up when she entered. Unable to stop herself, a sob escaped at seeing her father. The man who'd just yesterday helped customers at the store, even carrying bundles out for them, now lay in the bed, all semblance of health gone. It was strange to see frailty in the man who, although never large, remained quick and robust her entire life.

Mitch looked up and stood. "Nora, I've been worried. I couldn't leave to look for you..." His eyes flew to her waistline. "Have you been injured? There's blood on your clothes."

It struck her to be thankful then that their mother was so overcome she'd not noticed it was blood. Nora shook her head. "I'm fine. It was Grayson who was shot. I was there. It's his blood on my clothing."

"Is he well?"

"He's being seen to by the doctor now. But yes, it seems he will recover, unless an infection sets in." She closed the distance between them and fell into Mitch's broad chest. "I'm sorry I wasn't here with you and Mother. Did you speak to him before he died?"

Mitch hugged her and tensed at her question. "No, I did not speak to him. It was only after Ma told me he'd been unwell last night that I came to check on him. When I found him here in bed, he was alive, but barely. He died shortly after I fetched the doctor."

The tears she'd been holding burst from her and Nora cried while holding on to her brother. Sobs racked her as sorrow for the loss of their endearing, gentle father washed through her. Mitch patted her back, his chest shuddering as he cried with her.

This was a day of endings. She'd killed the cause of many nightmares. The one consolation in what she did was that her brother was free to live his life without worrying about the man harming her again. But what a price to pay. She'd killed, taken a human life. Was that why God took her father's? Sobs racked through her so hard, it hurt and yet she continued, not able to stop.

"What will happen to Mother, Mitch? Who will see to her every whim?" Nora brushed tears away.

"Don't worry about that now. We'll wait and see what she wishes to do."

That evening, after Carolyn Banks was tucked in the guest bedroom after taking a sedative and Mitch slept in the family room, Nora left the house and went to check on Grayson. She'd bathed and changed her clothes, yet the stench of the man's touch seemed to remain. Somehow, she'd have to broach the subject of her shooting the stranger with Mitch. He'd hear about it sooner or later from a townsperson and would confront her. She'd rather he learn about it from her.

Doctor Dougherty looked up as she walked in, his lips curved into a polite smile. "How are you, Nora? Did your mother take the sedative I left?"

"Yes," Nora replied and motioned past him. "Can I see Grayson?"

"Of course. He's been sleeping, but doing well so far. His brother plans to take him home tomorrow. He went to get Bronson and a cart."

Grayson lay in the darkened room. A soft snore told that he slept and she smiled at the sound. Closing the distance, she leaned over him and checked his coloring. As if sensing her regard, he took a deep breath and turned his face towards her. Unable to stop herself, she pressed a kiss to his mouth, enjoying the softness of his lips.

"You have to get well, Grayson. I need you."

A tear slipped down her cheek and she wiped it away. "As stubborn as you are, I know you prefer not to be lying about like this."

His lips twitched, but he remained asleep and she sat to watch over him for a few minutes.

Chapter Fifteen

Ashley returned to town on the cart with Bronson beside him. His brother was unusually somber keeping his eyes straight ahead, his brow furrowed.

"He's going to be all right," Ashley said, in an attempt to reassure Grayson's twin. "Doc said the only thing to watch for is fever."

Bronson nodded and took a breath. "I know. It's just that he could've died. I should have come to see about him, to help out with your situation."

"You're here now." Ashley placed a hand on his brother's shoulder. "Let's get our brother home and take care of him."

The sheriff waved them over and Ashley considered not paying heed. Instead, he pulled the horse to a stop and handed the reins to Bronson. "Go on to Doc's, I will meet you there in a few minutes."

"Are you sure?"

He ignored Bronson's concern and motioned with both hands for him to go. "I'll be there shortly. Don't move him until I get there."

Sheriff Dawson watched Bronson leave before speaking. "After talking with Nora Banks and investigating all this mess, I've decided you had nothing to do with Walters' murder."

Instead of saying something that would get him in more trouble, Ashley remained silent.

"But there is the matter of your treatment of Grace. She claims not to be hurt, but I've seen her favor that right arm." His narrowed eyes looked over Ashley. "You're lucky I'm not going to do anything about it right now with what's going on with your brother and all. But you watch yourself, Ashley Cole. Walk a straight line. I got my eye on you."

"One day I'll figure out why you hate me so much, Uncle Miles."

The sheriff turned and went back into his office without replying.

It was three blocks to the doctor's office. Ashley went past the mercantile and saw a *"Closed due to death in the family"* sign on the door. He wondered when it would be a good time to tell Grayson that Nora's father had passed. Perhaps it would be something better handled by their parents.

Once inside the doctor's office, he found Bronson sitting right inside the door. His eyes slid toward the back room and Ashley stalked back past the doctor who remained at his desk, head bent over a book.

Grayson was asleep. Nora held his hand while her head lay on the side of the bed and she, too, slept. Ashley approached and touched her shoulder.

Her eyes flew open and she looked first to Grayson and then up to Ashley. "Oh goodness, I must have dozed off." The beautiful woman stood and stretched her neck from side to side. "I came last night after mother finally fell asleep. I didn't plan to say all night." Her eyes went back to Grayson. "He's got a slight fever, but Doc doesn't seem too worried about it."

"Ma will take care of him. She's chomping at the bit to get him home."

Nora wiped her hands down her black skirts. "Yes, of course. Take care of him, Ashley." After patting Grayson's shoulder and kissing his brother's forehead, Nora went toward the door.

"I know you have the funeral and all to see to, but it would do Grayson good to see you. So please come out as soon as you can."

Nora kept her back to him. "Grayson and I are no longer engaged, Ashley. I'm sure he'll recover well enough without me visiting." She continued moving. Seconds later, the sound of the front door closing was followed by Bronson and the doctor coming into the back room.

Two weeks later.

"Ma, I really can't eat another bite." Grayson hated that he sounded more like a boy than a man, but his mother was relentless in feeding him constantly. She'd just shown up with cake and coffee even though he'd just eaten an hour earlier. He took the coffee to appease her and drank, unable to refuse her at noting the worry marks on both sides of her tight lips. "Can you take the stitches out? They're itching."

"Doctor Dougherty insists on coming out here tomorrow to check you before removing the stitches. I think it's best. The wounds, especially the one on your side, were deep."

Grayson attempted to sit straighter and grimaced, the pain was still unbearable at times. Bit he was tired of remaining flat on his back. Bronson, who'd walked in a minute earlier, helped by pushing an extra pillow behind his back and sat on a chair watching him.

"I'll be back to check on you later." Their mother placed the cake on the bedside table and left.

Grayson looked up at the ceiling and let out a breath. "I wish she wouldn't worry so much."

"You're lucky, Gray. The man could've killed you. We're all aware of that." Bronson's pained expression brought guilt over what his family went through because of him. He should've been more careful. "I know, but I'd do it again for Ashley."

"Nora hasn't been by to see you. It's been two weeks since you were shot."

He studied his brother's face for signs of anger or resentment, but all he saw was curiosity. "She's got enough to worry about with her father's passing and all. Besides, I'm not sure where we stand. Her father broke off the engagement."

"Yeah, he came here and talked to Pa. It was obvious his wife put the man up to it by the way he kept apologizing. Pa told him it should be up to you and Nora, but Mister Banks was insistent."

Grayson nodded. "It's what I told Nora when she told me." He stopped talking, realizing his brother would be pained to hear more.

"She cares for you, Grayson," Bronson said looking him straight in the eye. "I'm resigned that she'll never have deep feelings for anyone but you."

"Where do you get that idea from?" Surely Bronson was trying to make him feel better because he'd been shot.

His brother pressed on. "I spoke to her, that day Nora came out here and you found her in the barn. I asked her why she'd not accepted me and she replied it was because I would constantly remind her of you."

"I don't know about that. I know she doesn't trust me and I'm not sure I blame her. I've told her several times I don't plan to ever marry again." Regardless of the words, the thought of not seeing her brought emptiness he'd not felt before.

Although Bronson's admission was good to hear, Grayson wondered if he could ever gain Nora's trust. And if he did, what would it matter. Each time he considered the fact that Nora was someone he could picture himself with long-term, fear rose its ugly head and constricted his chest until he couldn't breathe.

Case in point, the stranger holding a gun to her temple

was proof of how fate could step in at any minute and snatch a loved one away.

Bronson got Grayson's attention by clearing his throat. "I have no idea how you felt when Sophia died, but I know it affected you a lot. If I could take that pain for you I would, Gray, just to see you happy again. The skirt chasin' and swagger about town is an act, a protection for your heart. We know it, the family. Nora's a good, beautiful woman and if you give it half a chance, you can be happy again. Don't let fear steal everything from you."

Grayson was speechless for a few minutes. Although he and Bronson had the uncommon bond of twins and could talk for hours about anything, for the first time he realized his brother was a wise man, someone he loved and admired, but had not given enough credit. "When did you get so smart?"

Bronson's lips lifted into his signature lazy smile, his face colored in a light blush. "Shut up, Gray."

"Come here, brother," Grayson said holding out his left arm. Bronson sat on the edge of the bed and they half-hugged. Bronson was careful not to hurt him.

"I love you." Bronson nudged his shoulder. "You scared the hell out of me, getting shot up like that."

"I love you, too. And believe me, it scared the hell out of me, too."

The brothers chuckled and Bronson lay back on the bed next to Grayson, his arms behind his head. "Remember when we used to pretend to get shot and make all those noises and motions before falling over?"

"Yeah, we were quite the actors," Grayson replied and shook his head. "I don't know if I made any noises when I got shot. Probably screamed like a woman."

"Nah, your voice is too deep, I'm sure you sounded more like a boar in heat." Bronson laughed at his own joke and grunted like a pig.

"Just remember we've got the same voice, so that's what you'd sound like, too."

Once again, his brother became somber. "Grayson, think about what I've said. You may lose Nora if you don't act. And that would be a tragedy."

The aromatic smell of coffee wafted through the door. It was time for his parents' nightly ritual of sitting at the dining room table to discuss the day over a cup of coffee. He pondered if he'd ever have that. Without warning, his heart began to pound and his breathing became erratic.

His twin watched with a solemn face, possibly able to understand what he went through, as they'd often deduced each other's feelings. "Take a deep breath, Gray, slow it down." Bronson's calmness helped and he clung to the words his brother repeated.

"You know," Bronson began once Grayson slumped back onto his pillow, his breathing under control. "There will come a time when you'll fear living without someone more than this irrational fear of hurting again. Once that happens, you will no longer allow fear to win."

They remained in the room, in a comfortable silence, Grayson deep in thought and Bronson at a small table, looking over the ranch's ledgers. Bronson's love for mathematics was a welcome gift since Ashley and their father preferred the outdoors to being cooped up in a room looking over the books.

Grayson's eyelids began to drop and he allowed sleep to take over. Later, through the haze of sleep, the bed moved and the pillows behind him were drawn away. Blankets were pulled over him and the lamplight went out. Although comforted by his caring family, a dull ache remained and his last coherent contemplation was if Nora thought about him this night.

Did she miss him?

The next day, the doctor arrived as expected. Grayson suffered through his mother's interrogation of the poor man, asking about each and every detail of what needed to be done to ensure he healed well. Just as his mother went to ask another question, he interrupted. "Ma, between my brothers and me, we've had more than enough broken bones, scrapes that needed stitches and remember that time Ashley got knocked out when he fell out of a tree? Why are you asking so many questions this time?"

Elizabeth Cole frowned at him. "None of you have been shot." Her hand reached up to her hair and she smoothed it back from her face. While he hated to stop her, at the same time he wondered about her overprotection. His mother was never one to pamper them.

"Should we proceed?" Doctor Dougherty looked to his mother. "Elizabeth, if you could assist me with..." They got busy with removing the stitches while Grayson concentrated on staring at the ceiling, breathing evenly to keep from jerking when the stitches were removed and the press of the doctor's fingers on his wounds sent cutting pains.

When the doctor moved away and began to pack up his bag, he looked to Grayson over his spectacles. "You can return to normal activities, but I advise you wait a couple weeks before riding." With an understanding smile, he looked to Elizabeth. "He's going to recover fully. I don't expect any complications whatsoever."

"I will see you out, doctor." Elizabeth Cole ushered him out and Grayson sat up gingerly, his side still tender. He pulled his shirt closed when his mother returned, her eyes downcast in thought.

"Grayson," she said, stopped to take a deep breath. "I need to tell you about something you probably don't remember." Her pretty face pinched. It was a grimace that made him wonder if she was in pain. When he went to stand, she held her hand out motioning him to stay. "Please, just let me talk."

"Ma, what's wrong."

Her half-smile failed to reassure him. "I know I've been overly protective and smothering you half to death. I'm sorry, honey. But you see, this is the second time I've almost lost you and I've been so afraid that having cheated fate once, it would come back for you."

"What do you mean?"

"When you and Bronson were but two years old, we lost you. We'd gone to Virginia City to take the three of you boys to the fair. I was holding your hand and suddenly you were gone."

Grayson searched his memory but could not remember the event. In silence, he waited for his mother to continue.

"Finally, I saw you a ways down the road. Your beautiful golden curls stood out in the distance. I was never so glad to have let your hair grow long in my life. I raced toward you after ensuring your father held on to your brothers." She sniffed and wiped her eyes with the back of her hand. "It was a woman. She picked you up and tucked you into a buggy, leaving before I could get to you. Just as she rode off, you turned and saw me. Started screaming and crying. Tore my heart to pieces, I collapsed on the ground screaming as loud as you."

Grayson took her hand and she continued. "Thankfully, several people got a good look at her. Your father and I searched nonstop, formed posses and traveled throughout the area until we found you two days later. She lived not too far from here. The woman was mad with grief. She'd lost her little daughter to typhoid and took you, thinking you were a girl."

Elizabeth Cole cupped his jaw. "It was a long time before you trusted me to leave you alone."

He finally understood his mother's doting on him and why she had such a problem cutting his hair. It was a security for her. Grayson took her hand. "Thank you, Ma. If it makes you feel any better, I promise to follow the doctor's instructions to the letter. It's comforting to know that you and Pa went to such lengths to find me."

Later that day, Grayson sat in front of the fireplace and

watched the rhythmic dance of the flames, the occasional crackle soothing.

His father and Bronson returned from outdoors and hung their gun belts and hats on pegs inside the doorway.

"Feeling better, son?" His father placed a large hand on Grayson's shoulder. "Stitches came out today, right?"

"Yes, I was going to come out to the barn, but Ma..."

"She'd not allow it," his father told him, understanding. "Yeah, well, there'll be plenty of time for that."

His brother walked past them, a grunt the only acknowledgment before he went up the stairs. Grayson drew his brows together. "Is he upset about something?"

"Your brothers had an argument today. They almost came to blows," his father said and sat down to tug his boots off. Ashley and Bronson often argued, both stubborn and not willing to give an inch, even if proven wrong.

"What did they fight over?"

A thump of a boot on the wooden floor was followed by a second and his father let out a happy sigh leaning back onto the soft chair and placing his stockinged feet up on a footstool. "I am not quite sure, something to do with who would be driving the cattle to Idaho next month. Ashley said something along the lines that Bronson should stick to the ledgers and your twin lost his temper and tackled him to the ground." Hank shook his head.

"I'd forgotten about the cattle drive."

"No matter, you're not going."

"Pa."

"No."

Chapter Sixteen

"Answer me, Nora." Mitch stretched forward, his hands gripping the edges of the table so hard that if the wood were a bit thinner it would most likely snap. Mitch's darkened eyes bore into her very soul. "Tell me why you were in the woods with a gun?"

They were in their parents' dining room. Although a hint of her lilac perfume remained, Carolyn Banks had long gone to her bedroom to retire for the night.

Nora dreaded having to relive the day of the shooting. Since then, every detail of the night she'd been attacked by the same man was once again fresh in her mind's eye. The episode, once again, dredged up nightmares that kept her awake in fear. Weary from lack of sleep for the last two weeks, she hadn't the strength to be anything but blunt with Mitch. Came right out and said, "I killed the man who shot Grayson. He would have killed us all if I hadn't."

No longer was it possible not to respond to her brother's demands and she reached across the table and cupped his face. "I love you so much, Mitch. One of the reasons I went out there was because of that. My heart was torn between my deep feelings for you and fear of what could happen to Grayson. I felt any other choice did not exist."

"Nora, please just tell me." His hands relaxed, but his upper body remained inclined forward, anticipating her next words.

"It was him. Once again, the man that attacked us came to upset our lives and I wasn't about to let him affect us in such a way that I'd lose you forever." Mitch blanched, but remained frozen, his eyes locked on her. Nora continued past her dry throat. "He came into the store the day before. Of course, he didn't recognize me, but I never forgot his voice. If you remember, it was the day I came out back at the mercantile and told you I was feeling ill."

Mitch nodded, but did not speak, his countenance urging her to continue.

Nora looked through the window and noticed it was a sunny day. Spring had arrived in full force. "When we went back inside, Grayson was there. He gave me a description of who he suspected killed Walters and I knew it was the same man. I told Grayson where I suspected the stranger's hideout was. Later, when I heard that Grayson formed a posse and went after him, there was no way I could stay here and do nothing."

"You should have told me, you could have been killed," Mitch told her, his voice quiet, full of hurt and reproach. "Once again, I failed to keep you safe."

"No!" Nora jumped from her seat and took her brother by the shoulders. Hoping to shake reason into him, she jerked him back and forth. "Don't you see? I am not the weak fifteen-year-old girl that was attacked. I didn't do it because I thought you couldn't defend me. I did it to prove to you that I am a strong, able woman who can take care of herself. I did it because I want you to live your life, Mitch, not to throw it away attempting to make up for that night. Please, Mitch, I want you to have a full life, get married, have a family. Be happy."

Nora collapsed into a chair, her left hand still on Mitch's shoulder. "It's time to let me go, Mitch. If you'd gone out there to that cabin, your mind would have been muddled with fury and it could have cost you your life."

"What about you?" His shoulders hunched. His posture tore her heart, but she forced the urge to be gentle back.

"I want to be free of your overprotectiveness. And you, well, you deserve to be free, too. I am going to move on. Figure out how to divide my time between the school and the mercantile. Perhaps allow the new teacher to take over most of the classes and gradually work my way to helping at the store on a permanent basis. Maybe I'll take up oils."

"You're a horrible artist." Although his voice remained flat, the barb helped alleviate the heaviness of their conversation.

"I'll take lessons," Nora quipped.

"I should be the one to take over the mercantile," Mitch told her with a half-smile. "You should marry Grayson and have children. If anyone can, you will get the scoundrel to settle down."

The mention of Grayson's name made her heart pitch. "As you are well aware, he and I are no longer engaged. He is not interested in marrying me."

"I wouldn't be so sure, sister. I see the way he looks at you. His eyes devour you. Grayson Cole is not at all indifferent to you, Nora."

No, Grayson was not indifferent to her. Nora had to admit that, in his own way, he cared for her, albeit as much as he was capable of caring for a lover, but not a wife. There was no desire to marry the man. "Perhaps he does care for me, Mitch, but Grayson does not plan to settle down anytime soon." She changed the topic of conversation, not wanting to discuss Grayson.

"Mother insists she'd rather live alone than have one of us move in." Nora chewed her bottom lip. "I am not sure that's the best. I should move in, especially if the new teacher takes over. She could use the cottage. It belongs to the town, after all."

Mitch was thoughtful. "Yeah, Ma is still in shock, not sure of where she stands now that Pa's gone."

The familiar room seemed darker, the dark wood paneling not allowing for enough light. The well-varnished furniture looming too large for the space. Her mother always favored dark woods and oversized cabinets. The two-story house was too large for a widow, but Carolyn Banks would never live anywhere else. "I will live here and remain with Mother."

"What if you get married, then what?" Mitch insisted.

A smile curved her lips. "If any potential suitor is not put off by our mother's ways and my lack of decorum, then I'm sure I'll be content to come up with a workable solution." She tapped her finger on her chin. "Maybe Mother can live with you and whoever your future wife is."

Mitch's lips twitched. He fought to keep from smiling and gave her a severe look. "That will not happen. I believe mothers are best suited for life with their daughters."

As only Mitch could, his mood shifted quickly and once again became solemn, his large hand covering hers. "Truthfully, Nora, are you all right? This second encounter must have jarred memories. You look tired."

"I am. And yes, I will not lie to you, I've been having nightmares. But when I wake, I am aware he is dead and will no longer hurt me. I take comfort that time will help alleviate it."

Her brother stood and stretched. "If you need anything..."

"I am fine. Go on." Nora stood and hugged her brother. Her arms around his waist, she laid her head on his chest. "I love you, Mitch."

"And I, you."

The stillness of the room after Mitch left surrounded her. Nora wondered of her future and what it would bring.

Her thoughts went to Grayson. Did he recover well from his injuries? He'd not been to town in the last few weeks or if he had, he'd avoided her. It was for the best. At least, that's what she wanted to believe.

She closed her eyes and pictured him once again kissing her. He was a wonderful kisser. Yet the memory that stuck out most was the darkening of his blue eyes when they locked to hers.

Would her hands ever again glide through his long, silky hair? If she ever did marry, would her husband remove these memories? Would time?

No. Never.

Two days later, Nora stood behind the counter at the mercantile. Miss Bixby, the new teacher insisted on taking over Nora's tasks to give her freedom to work at the mercantile until her mother was out of mourning. She'd never return to the school. Both she and Miss Bixby knew that, but it was gracious of her to stop by earlier that day and give Nora a report of the students' progress while at the same time asking questions to ensure all their needs were met.

The bell over the door jingled and Grayson Cole strolled in, his eyes immediately searching her out. Her heart skipped then fell to her stomach. Unsure how to greet him, she settled for devouring the sight of him. Mitch stopped Grayson's progress and the men spoke in hushed tones. Grayson, just a bit taller than Mitch was able to look over at her on occasion.

"I'd like a bag of sugar, please."

"Oh, of course. I'm sorry Miss Bunch." Nora blinked at the customer she'd momentarily forgotten. Turning, she reached for the package from the shelf behind her. Once the woman paid and departed with the parcels, Nora was once again free to observe Grayson.

His broad shoulders moved up and down as he replied to whatever Mitch inquired of him. With a composed expression, eyes flat, he seemed to be explaining something to her brother. Nora itched to move closer and hear what they spoke about, but didn't dare. Mitch turned to her and then motioned for Grayson to go out the front door with him.

Without looking at her, Grayson did as her brother bid. Disappointed he'd left so soon, she leaned on the counter and released a breath. What could they be discussing?

Chapter Seventeen

"Damn it, Mitch, I don't know what you want me to say."
Grayson wanted nothing more than to go back inside and
take Nora away for a few hours, spend time with her. It had
become impossible to stay away and not see her, and now
her brother stood before him asking his intentions toward
his sister.

While noble and understandable, Grayson could not
answer the question in a manner that would suit Mitch.
How could he explain that, although he did not plan to
marry, he wanted to at least be able to spend time with
Nora? He needed it. He craved her company.

"I am aware that our father broke the engagement with
your family," Mitch explained slowly. "If you plan to renew
that arrangement, I would like to know. If not, then why do
you seek out Nora? She's been through enough."

Did she not want to see him? Had she asked her
brother to intercede? "Did she ask you to stop me?"
Grayson snapped, losing patience. "I came to talk to her, to
thank her for what she did out there."

"No, she did not ask me to stop you. And very well, go
on." Mitch finally relaxed his pose. "But I warn you,
Grayson, don't hurt my sister."

"That is the last thing I wish to do." And he meant it.

Nora would be the woman he'd want to marry, if he could. As hard as he tried to forget, she was present in every moment, invading not only his thoughts, but his dreams as well.

They entered the store and she looked up. She was bent over, next to a bin of fabric. Her amber gaze shifted between her brother and Grayson. Mitch moved to stand behind the counter, seeming to busy himself with items that needed arranging. He gave them his back.

"Can I speak to you for a few moments?" Grayson neared, fighting every instinct to pull her against him. "I brought the wagon. I thought we could go for a short ride." He glanced over at Mitch and met the brother's solid stare. "Only if you wish, Nora."

"I—I," Nora stuttered and looked to her brother. Mitch nodded in agreement. "Very well." She removed her apron and folded it before placing it aside.

Grayson proffered his arm and she slipped her hand into the crook, resting it on his forearm. The simple touch sent his heart racing and he allowed his lips to curve when looking at her as he escorted her outside.

After assisting her to sit, he rounded the wagon and climbed onto the bench. Already, the day looked brighter, every noise cheerful. Grayson snapped the reins, eager to get away from the curious townsfolk's glances.

They rode for a few minutes without speaking until finally Nora turned to him. "Where are we going?"

"It's just up here a few miles. We'll go see my land. I want to check on it, make sure no one has set up a homestead."

"Ah." Nora's unemotional reply unsettled him. He looked over to see her looking straight ahead, the picture of calmness and reserve.

He pulled the horses to a stop once he arrived at the destination and climbed down, rounding to help Nora. She looked across the clearing, her eyes taking in every detail. His chest expanded with pride at the land he'd purchased with his own earnings. The meadow was replete with wildflowers. A brook nearby fed the plentiful trees that flourished. A bird cawed overhead announcing its presence as several others joined in its rustic song. Thankfully, there was a warm breeze which made the sunny day perfect for early spring.

"Come." He took Nora's elbow and guided her around the wagon after pulling a blanket from the back in case she wanted to sit. "I want to show you the brook. It's clear and runs deep."

They walked towards the water, his heart lifting at her cry of delight at spotting the gurgling creek. "Oh, Grayson, it's so beautiful here."

She kneeled and cupped her hands bringing the cool water to her face. "I had no idea this place existed."

When he remained silent, her beautiful amber eyes rose to him. With wisps of hair surrounding her face, the sunlight gave her an angelic appearance. Lips pursed, she studied him for a moment. "You planned to build a house here with your wife, didn't you?"

It was easy to tell from the way he took in the surroundings just how much this place meant to him. His bright blue eyes scanned her face then lifted to skim over the surrounding land. "Yes, I did actually. It's over there, past this grove. It's not finished yet. I cleared a lot of trees just on the other side there." He pointed to where several of the felled trees still remained.

"Are you going to finish building one day?"

Grayson scowled. She wondered if he'd snap at her. Instead, he sunk to the ground and placed the blanket he carried next to him. "I'm not sure."

An honest answer and she appreciated it. Nora went to him and spread the blanket before sitting upon it. "Why did you come for me today, Grayson? It only makes it harder for me."

"I miss you. Talking to you, seeing you," Grayson told her and reached forward to cup her face.

How she'd missed him as well, but at the same time, she'd not dared to hope to be this near to him again. "Kiss me." Her blurted request took them both by surprise. "Oh goodness, Grayson, you don't have to."

With reverent care, his hands held her face and he smiled at her. "It's what I've dreamed of doing since that night at your home." His mouth took hers, tentatively at first. The soft press of his lips over hers was unexpected for him, but at the same time, sweet. He coaxed her forward, his hand sliding down her shoulders. Nora moaned when his lips traced a leisurely trail down her jawline to her throat and threaded her fingers through his hair.

When he pulled back, she opened her eyes to his now darkened ones. She would not let this moment end so quickly. Drawing from instinct alone, she slid her hand down his chest to stop at the top of his belt, then to the side until her palm rested on his thigh.

His eyes followed her movements, his breathing altered from their kiss and her machinations. Next, she trailed a finger from her other hand to his throat, circling it playfully around his exposed throat then down to where the top button of his shirt was undone. His chest lifted with a deep breath, but he did not move to stop her. Instead, he watched her intently. Nora leaned and placed a kiss right beneath his jawline, allowing her lips to linger on his quickening pulse.

Emboldened when his hand moved to the back of her neck, she flicked her tongue out and licked the spot where her lips lifted.

"Ahh." The hoarse sound escaped from Grayson. "God, Nora, you're driving me crazy."

She slid her hand up from his thigh to the juncture of his legs and whispered into his ear. "I want you, Grayson. I don't want to think about the future or circumstances. I just want to feel."

Grayson fell back onto the blanket and she pounced on the opportunity. The power of bringing the beautiful man to a tremble aroused her until she could barely stop trembling herself. This man never failed to surprise her, and did so once again by giving her complete access to his body, trusting her to explore him without making her feel foolish. She tightened the hold on him and his hips lifted.

A large hand covered hers, his breath now in pants. Grayson lifted his head and smiled at her. "I cannot hold back much longer." One side of his mouth lifted in a crooked smile inviting her to once again cover his mouth with hers.

He pushed her back and rolled her gently until they lay side by side. They looked at each other, their faces almost touching. "I don't know what I can offer you, Nora."

Before he could continue, she placed a finger over his lips. "No talk." Where the boldness came from, she'd ponder later. Nora stood and without taking her eyes from Grayson, she removed her clothing. With an expression that could only be described as awe, he watched her without moving. When all her clothes were finally gone, he rose. With tentative movements he neared and placed his hands on her waist.

Nora fell against his broad chest, the contrast of her nudity against his fully dressed body made her actions even more wanton, more daring and she did not regret it one bit, especially when his large hands cupped her bottom and he pulled her against his hardness. His mouth trailed once again from her mouth to her neck and finally between her breasts, the heat of his breath against her skin while his tongue licked the valley. Nora's head fell back and, with closed eyes, she took in his every motion, committing them to memory.

Sensations overwhelmed her senses until all Nora could do was to hold on to his shoulders to keep from toppling over. With tender care, he laid her onto the blanket and rose to disrobe.

Somehow, Nora managed to keep her eyes open to see each inch of Grayson displayed for her. First his shirt slid from his broad shoulders, down his arms to fall onto the ground. He was magnificent. Even the sunlight could not keep from touching his body, reflecting from the golden skin, giving the illusion of a glow coming from him. His now healed gunshot wounds caught her attention next. The one on his lower abdomen, a ragged scar, added appeal to his otherwise unmarred skin.

Grayson lowered to lie beside her and pulled her against him. The color of his eyes, once again, a different shade of blue, this time reminiscent of the ocean. "I want you, Nora. I want you to be sure."

"I am sure."

Nora gasped and took his face in her hands for a second to look into his eyes before Grayson took her mouth with savage hunger. The urgency continued between them, an experience she would commit to memory as she knew it was the last time she'd be with a man. Grayson would be her only lover. She'd move on, but this was her gift to herself and although improper and against every rule, it was worth breaking them.

His large body covered hers and the upward spiral began and Nora thrashed under Grayson, emotions swirling with the physical excitement until she thought she'd burst into a thousand pieces. Falling over the crest, she heard the faint sounds of lovemaking, followed by her high-pitched cry and his deeper roar.

They lay in each other's arms until their breathing settled. Grayson took her face in his large hands and kissed her with soft lips. "My Nora." His eyes finished the caress, moving ever so slowly across her features.

Moments later, Grayson jerked to sit, hand on his chest and his breath sounding like gasps. Nora reached for him and he moved away from her touch. "I can't...."

"What's wrong?" She sat up and caught the pure fear in his contorted face. "Grayson?"

He closed his eyes inhaling deeply. He turned to her and kissed her again. This kiss felt like detachment. Too soon, Grayson regained control and once again his façade, the one he wore to keep people at a distance, returned.

He pulled her against his side. "We should be heading back. Your brother will worry."

"Yes, of course." Nora pushed away to get up, but he held her in place and pulled her face up so she could meet his gaze.

"Thank you."

What was she supposed to say? You're welcome seemed trite. Why was he thanking her when she'd initiated what had transpired between them? There were no words, only the knowledge that he'd never be hers and this was the last time they'd be together. She managed a smile and once again moved away. This time he allowed it.

They dressed mostly in silence. Grayson finished first and moved a distance away to look over the water, his face tight, emotionless.

Nora went to stand beside him. "I can see why you love this land. I hope one day you do build a house here and raise a family."

His face swung to hers and he traced a finger down her nose. "You're beautiful, Nora. I don't think I've told you how often those whiskey-colored eyes of yours appear in my thoughts. I'm not sure what I'll do about this land." Abruptly he changed topic, his attention now away from her. He focused across the treetops. "My brothers are leaving on a cattle drive. I'll be helping Ma at the ranch. I won't be around town for a few months."

"Of course," Nora said and sighed, studying the horizon before her. "I'm sure you will build on this land, Grayson," she told him, her heart breaking at the thought. Senseless jealousy filled her so it hurt physically causing a slash of pain to crisscross her chest. "One day, you'll meet a woman who will make it so hard to live without her, you'll no longer avoid moving on."

He cocked a brow, a soft curve to his lips. "Always thinking aren't you, Nora?" Once again, he looked across the water. "Moving on. I don't know about that. But one day, I will do something with this land. Maybe the thought of settling down will not be such a bad thing."

Grayson escorted her to the mercantile entrance. He rode around to the back to load the items he'd come to get for the Cole ranch and, before long, he left. Nora floated through the few remaining hours, barely able to keep from running away to a place where she could scream and cry until the pain that choked her airway ebbed. Her brother constantly slid glances at her, but didn't say anything. Mitch, who'd usually not allow her to mope about without asking questions, seemed subdued and deep in his own thoughts. Thank goodness.

Finally, they closed up shop and returned home. She immediately sought her bedroom, claiming a headache to avoid dinner. She felt horrible at not taking time for her mother, who still mourned. But this day, Nora did not have any strength left for anyone else. Tears spilled down her cheeks as soon as she crossed the threshold and she stumbled to the bed, falling into it. Sobs raked her entire body. Fearing her mother would overhear, she buried her face into the pillow to silence them.

Grayson was gone. When she'd see him again, he'd either be stopping by the store for provisions or seeking another female's companionship in town. But never would he pursue her. Never again would he come for her. The excuses he'd used were not foreign to her. Although she'd never been in a relationship, she'd heard the stories of woe from other women. Besides that, her instincts told her she'd be better off if she let him go.

If only her heart could.

One thing she was thankful for was that he was honest to a fault. He had ensured she understood where they stood. The words he'd spoken, perhaps not knowing how deeply they'd sunk a knife in her heart, had firmly built a thick wall between them. One so high and thick it was impossible to tear down.

It was dark outside when she was able to stop crying. Nora got up from the bed and went to the window to look to the stars glistening in the sky. Every day that passed would help her move forward, the pain would fade.

But her love for Grayson Cole would remain, unfortunately for her. For years now, he'd become entrenched forever in her foolish heart.

Chapter Eighteen

Ashley didn't want to risk running into Sheriff Dawson by walking in front of the jailhouse. The man did not like him and would take any opportunity to throw him back in jail.

He waited for a horse-drawn wagon loaded high with sacks of grain to pass and then crossed the dusty street.

It wasn't his idea to be in town today, but Bronson was deep in the ledgers, ensuring all was set for their departure and Grayson left early with their father to round up the cattle, so his mother insisted he go to town and collect any mail that may have arrived at the train station.

He shook his head knowing she'd ordered some fabrics and catalogs and was anxious to get her hands on them.

There was a lot to do before leaving and he intended on making this trip a quick one. But it seemed fate had other plans for him this day. Halfway to town his horse threw a shoe, so he rode at a slow pace making the two-hour trip almost four. He'd taken the horse to the blacksmith who informed him it would be a couple hours since he was finishing work for someone else. Until his horse was shod, he decided to walk around and look for something to occupy his time. After stopping at the mercantile to order provisions, he went outside to wait in the shade from the awning over the seamstress' doorway.

Ashley leaned against the wall and scanned down the street. A group of people exited the hotel. He recognized the lady, a friend of his mother's. Next to her, an older man, her husband, stood and held her elbow. The man with them made the air leave his lungs. Captain Ford, his commander from the cavalry.

Ashley pulled his hat down but kept an eye on the group. What the hell was Ford doing in Alder Gulch?

As if sensing he was watched, Ford looked up, his shrewd eyes scanning until resting on a pair of ladies who'd stopped and watched the newcomer with ill-disguised interest. Of course, the man caught women's eyes. He was tall, commanding and golden. The blond male nodded to the women in acknowledgement and then looked directly at Ashley.

Ashley maintained his relaxed stance, not giving the impression that he noticed Ford's attention. Ford continued his perusal along the street.

The bell over the seamstress' door rung and Ashley shuffled to avoid whoever exited. Damn, even if his horse was ready, he had to wait for the group, who continued in a leisurely conversation, to leave.

"If you're not going to move out of my way, I'm going to kick you." The familiar voice got his attention. Grace's dark, narrowed gaze pinned him.

For a moment, he was speechless at her appearance. Dressed in a brilliant green gown with a low cut bodice, her midnight black hair was up in a complicated hairstyle, some curls escaping down to her shoulders. She was stunning.

Why had he not noticed her beauty before? Frozen on the spot, his gaze swept from her skirts past her small waist to the swell of her breasts to her face. Grace cocked an impatient eyebrow at him. Ashley cleared his throat and grabbed the pile of parcels from her gloved hands. "I apologize, didn't realize I was blocking the doorway."

"Give me those." She made to take them, but he turned away.

"Allow me to escort you to your buggy." What the hell was he doing? Unable to stop himself, he attempted a rare smile at the stunned woman. "I owe you an apology and it's the least I can do."

Her brows drew together and, for a second, he thought she'd rebuff him, but instead she surprised him by slipping her hand through his arm with an indignant huff. "I don't know what's worse, allowing the man who escaped jail after manhandling me, as an escort, or standing here arguing while people watch us."

His blood ran cold. He looked over and straight into Ford's direct gaze. The captain's barely visible nod was the acknowledgment he got in return. He'd been recognized.

Ashley felt a tug and realized he'd stepped on Grace's skirts.

"Confounded dress, this is why I don't normally wear all this." She motioned to her dress with her free hand. "I don't know how women manage to walk around all day in this damn garb." She continued her unladylike mumbling while walking alongside him. Her presence and prickly personality calmed his rapid heartbeat and he was thankful for it.

"Why are you wearing it then?" he found himself asking.

Grace looked up and her lips curved. Ashley could not help but notice the full lips, definitely meant for kissing. A slight frown formed and she sighed. "There's going to be some reception in the hotel in a couple hours. Father says it's for a distinguished cavalry captain who is considering moving here. My father wants to retire next year and devote his time to our ranch, so he's contriving a plot to get the captain to run for sheriff."

"I see," were the only words he could utter, once again the blood in his veins chilling.

They stopped next to her buggy and she extricated her

hand from his arm. The absence of her warm touch left him colder. After taking the packages, she placed them on the floorboard.

"Thank you, Ashley Cole." Grace started to turn and he stopped her with a hand on her forearm.

"Wait." What could he say to warn her? For some strange reason, he needed to keep this woman safe. "Look, I know you don't know me well or have any reason to trust me, but can you promise me something?" He glanced across the street to see the captain and his group had finally left.

Her eyebrows lifted and she nodded. "What?"

"Don't allow that man near you. Stay away from Captain Ford."

"You know him?"

Again, scanning the street, Ashley noted the captain was gone. "I—yes, I do."

Her gaze slid away. She nibbled at her bottom lip and then released the moistened morsel. It took Ashley's entire resolve to tear his eyes away. "I'm not sure that warning is necessary. Not only can I take care of myself, but I have no intention of letting any man near me."

Ashley lifted an eyebrow at her and she huffed. "You forced yourself on me today."

"It was easy to escape when you were my captor, so I'm not so sure you are as tough as you think."

She pressed her lips together into a thin line and her brows lowered.

A moment later, her face changed, softened. Grace's eyes lifted to meet his, her lips pursed into a bow. She leaned forward and Ashley could not help but follow her lead.

Pain exploded on both his foreleg and face when she managed to kick his shin and slap him at the same time. "You are not a nice person, Ashley Cole."

With a swish of skirts, she rounded her buggy. He watched in fascination as she wrestled with her dress to climb into the seat. By the time she settled, her hair was askew and there was a visible tear in the hem. Head high and chin jutted, she snapped the reins, setting the startled horses into a quick trot.

Ashley rubbed at his face. It had been a long time since someone caught him by surprise. The mood vanished when he stared across the street toward the smithy's shop. If Captain Ford became sheriff, his life would change drastically and not for the good.

Some things from the past were best left buried. With Ford's arrival, a multitude of cruel things returned to haunt him.

That night at the bunkhouse, Ashley sat on his bunk and stared at the wall, his mind awhirl. What would he do now? He would not leave his family.

He'd not gone to dinner at the house that night. It would have been too hard to get away with his current dark mood. His mother would know something bothered him.

Tomorrow, there would be no excuse. But tonight, he had to come up with a way to find out what Ford planned.

The soft rap at the door made him groan. "Yeah!"

"Hank Ashley Cole, what are you doing sitting in the dark?" His mother swept into the room, her soft, floral fragrance managing to reach him despite the otherwise stale smell of the space. Her fiery eyes trained on him. He couldn't help but notice the beauty she still remained. "I asked you a question."

"I'm not fit to be around people, Ma," Ashley said, rising to get a chair for his mother. When he placed it in front of his bunk, she ignored it and continued to stand.

"I'm so tired of it, Ash, of this dark cloud that surrounds you." She shook her head. "Tell me, son, what happened to you? What made you change so much? What are you battling?" Her worried gaze fell over him and Ashley attempted to find a reasonable reply. When an answer didn't come, he sat on the edge of the bed and slumped forward, elbows on his knees.

"Ashley?" His mother cupped his chin and lifted his face. "Talk to me. This has gone on long enough, son. We can't help you if we don't know what troubles you so."

When he met her gaze, the unshed tears made his gut clench. "Ma, don't." He turned from her. "I have been through things, done things I could never tell you. Terrible things. I can't share them with you or anyone."

"Don't you dare tell me how to feel," his mother yelled. "Look at me." Ashley turned to his mother's reddened face.

She let out a breath. "There is nothing in this world that I love more than you and your brothers. If I could take this pain from you and carry it, I would. It breaks my heart to see you so tormented. But I have faith in that you are a strong man, Ashley. You can do something about it. Do you understand me?"

Tears threatening, Ashley could only nod in response. He attempted to tell her he loved her, but his throat constricted.

"Now," his mother said peering down at him. "You will talk to me or your father. Even one of your brothers if that's easier. Just a little bit each day. Share something, anything. You have to let go of whatever it is, no matter how terrible. We will love you through the healing. You understand?"

He nodded and she leaned and kissed his check. "Good night, son. Sleep well."

When the door sounded behind his mother, Ashley lounged back onto the bunk and let his eyes close. Tears managed past his eyelid and trailed down the side of his face.

If only he could share everything. Even the parts he refused to think about. It was hard enough to accept the horrible things that happened to him while he'd been under the command of Captain Erwin Ford. To put it into words was impossible.

Chapter Nineteen

Spring was in full bloom. The flowering trees added a burst of color to the otherwise green landscape of Alder Gulch. Nora closed the front door of her mother's house and stepped into the bright afternoon sun. Thank goodness for a day of rest, otherwise she'd go mad from being indoors on this beautiful day. Her mother had insisted she stay home, strange that her usually self-absorbed mother noted Nora's subdued moods as of late. Perhaps she thought her overly tired from working at the mercantile or even from missing the children at the schoolhouse. Whatever the reason, Carolyn Banks insisted Nora take time to spend the day away from the store and the hustle and bustle of town. She even suggested Nora go for a ride, which her mother usually saw as unladylike.

An eye towards the mercantile, she considered going to work. No matter how enticing a day outdoors would be, eventually her thoughts would roam to the usual and saddening memories of her last time with Grayson.

Olivia promised to stop by as soon as her chores at the clinic were over and they'd go for a ride in her buggy. The light breeze caressed her face and she closed her eyes and inhaled. Perhaps a few moments sitting in of her father's rocker would suffice for the moment. Nora lowered into the worn comfortable chair, a smile tugged at her lips remembering how often she'd found him sitting here smoking his pipe, holding a bag of candy for any children that happened by. Of course, the local kids did make it a point to stop by.

"Good morning, Nora." The familiar, deep voice brought her heart to a gallop until she looked up and saw Bronson. Humor-filled blue eyes met hers and, for a second, she wondered if he knew she'd expected to see his brother. "You seem to be enjoying the day."

Nora motioned for him to sit opposite her in the other rocker and he did, his large body filling the chair. A comfortable ease that normally came from being around Bronson filled her. Genuinely liking him, she was glad he stopped by, as she'd not seen him since the fair at his ranch. "I'm glad to see you returned from the cattle drive. Did it go well?"

When he smiled, two deep dimples formed in his cheeks, a distinguishing factor between the twins. She thought his eyes were different too. Bronson's seemed lighter than Grayson's, almost grey in appearance. "I'm glad to be back. It wasn't too bad, but we did get a couple of rainstorms that had us living like pigs in mud for a few days."

"Oh, I bet that got uncomfortable," Nora replied and chuckled. "How are your parents and brothers?"

He lifted an eyebrow at her. "My parents are both well. Ma said Pa ain't allowed to go on any more drives. Seems she really missed him." He paused and looked away from her. "Grayson is doing well. He's here. Over at the mercantile."

Although her stomach pitched, she managed to keep from turning toward the store. "I bet he's glad you're back. You two are always a welcome sight in town with your similar looks and horses to match. Did Ashley come as well?"

Bronson's demeanor sobered. "No, he refuses coming

to town. Going through one of them dark spells. You know how my brother is."

"Yes, a loner. But Ashley is a good man," Nora replied, meaning it.

"Thank you for saying so. He is." Bronson stood. "I just stopped by when I saw you sitting here, but I better get going. Picking up some shirts Ma ordered for us. Take care, Nora." Bronson touched the tip of his hat and strolled away whistling.

A smile formed at considering how his behavior around her changed and it made her glad for it. She'd always liked Bronson and was happy to keep his friendship.

Nora rose and turned to the mercantile, not sure if she was thankful for not working today. Seeing Grayson again was inevitable. Sooner or later, she'd run into him, yet right now she was not ready to face him and not be affected. No, she did not have the strength. With a lift of her skirts, she went back inside into the dim interior of the house.

The words on the page of her book were not clear, not that it mattered. She wasn't reading it, not really. For who knew how many times, she once again reread the paragraph only to lift her eyes to the door. Should she go out and risk running into Grayson? Although she'd opened the curtains, the sunlight was not as alluring inside as it had been outdoors.

She turned back to the page and attempted to read once again when the sound of an approaching buggy got her attention. Still, the knocks on the door made her drop the book onto the floor with a hollow thump.

Her lips curved. Of course, Olivia promised to stop by and here she was. Crazy from being stuck inside, she was glad to get out with her friend. A smile on her face, she opened the door and gasped.

His face shadowed from the sun behind him and the

hat he wore made it hard to tell what his expression was. Grayson loomed in the doorway, completely filling it. "Hello, Nora."

She stepped back with a sharp breath. His arm reached around her and crushed her to him. The familiar scent of him and the hard body against hers almost brought her to tears. She lifted her face to tell him to release her, but his mouth covered hers with a hungry urgency that silenced her words. On the contrary, her body screamed for more.

His mouth ravished hers while he walked her backwards into the house, the door closing firmly behind them. Her lips parted and his tongue moved in to take even more from her. At the same time, she dug her fingers through his shoulder-length hair, enjoying the feel of the silky tresses. A deep moan escaped Grayson.

Nora clung on to his shoulders, savoring the taste of peppermint he'd obviously just eaten. When his lips slid to the corner of her mouth, he moved his hands to the small of her back. Trailing kisses to her ear, he pressed a soft kiss behind it.

"I miss you, Nora," Grayson whispered into her now highly sensitive lobe that tingled with the warmth of his breath. "Can't stop thinking about you."

"Grayson," Nora was breathless, "I can't do this. We..."

His mouth took hers again, his tongue plunging back in and silencing whatever she would say. Truth be told, she wasn't sure what she planned to tell him.

Placing both hands on either side of his face, she pushed his hair back and lifted him away. "Grayson, what are you doing?"

His now kiss-swollen lips curved. "I'm kissing you."

"Not that." She attempted not to smile, but failed. "I mean you and me, we're no longer engaged. I thought you planned to move on after what you said last time."

Both eyebrows lifted and he blinked several times. "What did I say?"

"Come outside, let's sit." Nora attempted to pull him

toward the door. It would be a horrible incident if her mother walked in on them while they groped each other without regard for propriety.

Unmoving, Grayson pulled her back against him. "I miss you." This time he pressed his forehead against hers and took a deep breath. "I don't know what do to about you."

"What do you mean?" Nora searched his face only to see confusion. "Grayson, you told me the thought of settling down was a bad thing."

A frown formed. "I did?"

"Yes," she insisted, taking his hand and attempting to pull him to the door. "You have to understand I won't continue in this type of a relationship with you. I live with Mother, now."

The stubborn cowboy moved toward her and she attempted to step away only to find herself against the wall. "This type?" His mouth went to her throat and the wicked tongue of his began to swirl against her skin, down to the top of her breast. Nora moaned and wrapped one arm around his shoulders and with her other hand held the back of his head.

His hard body held her a willing prisoner while he took his time tasting every inch of her exposed skin. Just as she was about to lose control, Grayson lifted his lips from her throat but continued to hold her against him. His breath came in short, hard pants and from the tenseness of his muscles, she could tell he fought for composure as much as she did.

"I'm sorry. I need a minute," he said, still breathless, not allowing her away from him. "I can't let you go." A resigned sound in his words, although soft.

"I don't know what you mean. Grayson, I'm trying my best to help you by not asking for anything, urging you to move on." Nora jerked away from his arms. "As long as you are not near, I can stay strong, but not when this happens." She motioned to the room with both arms. No longer caring that he knew everything. It was time for her to tell him exactly how she felt. "I cannot be indifferent to you, Grayson. I care too much. I always have. But now, after what's happened between us, every time we come together you take a piece of me when you leave."

He stood stock-still. The only part of him that moved was his chest with every breath. Darkened eyes locked to her. She commanded his rapt attention.

"Don't you see?" she continued, "I'm not angry with you for you've always been honest and clear. You have no intention of marrying me, which, although hard to accept, my head understands. But my heart doesn't, Grayson." Nora tore her eyes from his face. "My heart wants you every day. I want to fall asleep to you and wake to you. I want to share my life with you and hold you, be with you every day."

Unwilling to see the rejection or listen to anything he'd say to assure her, Nora rushed to the front door and threw it open. "Please, leave."

He stepped away and turned to the door. "I don't want to stop seeing you. Give me time to work things out, Nora." He took her hand and put it up to his face, his eyes boring into hers. "That's all I'm asking you for, time. I know I have many faults. My reputation as a womanizer is justified. But I promise you, I haven't been with anyone since you. I'm trying. Don't give up on me. Not yet. Please, Nora."

Breath left her body at the mixture of fear and pleading emanating from the normally distant man. "I don't...know what to say."

"Say you'll give me a chance. Say we're still engaged. Knowing how you feel for me makes me want to try harder. To be a better man for you."

Before she could reply, he neared and placed a soft kiss on her lips. "Come to supper at my parents' tomorrow. I'll come get you." A genuine smile lit up his gorgeous face and Nora could not help but return it.

"All right. I will."

"Good. That's good." Grayson seemed almost nervous when he stepped onto the porch and retrieved his hat from the floorboards. "You knocked it off my head when you threw yourself at me," he informed her. She gave him a playful look.

"Grayson Cole, I did no such thing." Nora enjoyed kidding with him. "Wait." She ran inside and grabbed her shawl. "Walk me to Olivia's house."

His eyebrows shot up and his chest visibly puffed. "I'd be proud to walk you anywhere you'd like. How about if we stroll past the mercantile first? That way I can ensure your mother is aware of the supper invite."

Nora nodded and smiled back. God, was it possible they'd actually make it work?

Grayson rode alongside Bronson who drove the wagon full of provisions from town.

The surprising turn of events after spending time with Nora lightened his mood. He'd planned to avoid her, but had practically run there after Bronson told him he'd visited her.

Her kisses, her plush body, had driven him crazy. If she'd but given any indication she was willing, he'd have taken her right there against the wall. Even remembering the hot kisses, her hands sliding down his back, took his breath.

Almost three months without seeing her had been torturous. He had planned to use the time away to ensure they no longer saw each other. His plan was to keep a distance if he ever ran into her, but it would be easier to cut off his own leg than to stay away from Nora Banks.

"You're in love." Bronson's statement shook him from his thoughts. "Just admit it and you'll feel better."

"What nonsense are you spouting about, brother?" Grayson shot a glare at his twin who smiled back.

"I said you're in love with Nora."

Grayson snorted, not ready to reply to his brother who, as usual, didn't know when to stop.

"I remember that look. Seen it before."

"Shut up, Bronson."

"Nope, not going to stop talking until you admit it. Hell, it's about time one of us seriously fell. Might as well be you."

"What about you? I thought *you* cared for her."

"Yeah, well, I still do, but not like you. If I'd had the opportunity to get closer to her, I have no doubt it would have happened. But it looks like you and her are meant to be."

"I'm sorry, brother," Grayson said, meaning it. "I'm not sure I deserve Nora. I'm trying to see if I can make a commitment to her, but that fear in my chest makes me stop breathing. I can't risk another time like with Sophia, I can't..."

Bronson pulled the wagon to a stop. The startled horses looked back to see what happened as he climbed from the wagon and motioned with one hand for Grayson to do the same.

Once they stood face to face, his twin placed his hand on Grayson's shoulder. "Be honest with me."

The grave expression took him aback. "I'm always honest with you. You're good at figuring out when I'm not."

His brother's scrutiny deepened. "What feels worse, right now? The fear of what could happen in the future or the thought of never seeing Nora again?"

Images of a bruised Nora, of burying her, the helplessness of not being able to do anything while she lay dying, were slowly overlapped by those of her walking arm in arm with him earlier, of her lush curves under his palms, her honey brown eyes sparkling when she'd accepted his invitation for dinner.

"She accepted to come for supper tomorrow," Grayson said stalling for time. "When I asked her, I thought she'd say no. Something began to squeeze in my chest. I thought she'd tell me to go and not come back. Ever."

"And when she accepted?" Bronson prompted.

"I could breathe."

"I'm right, then."

"God, Bronson, I do love her."

Bronson laughed. "Your expression of terror is more of a man told he's gonna hang in the morning than one who realized how lucky he is."

"I shouldn't be scared."

His brother's calm smile filled him with love for the one person he felt closest to. "No, Gray, you shouldn't be scared. You deserve to feel happy, excited. Look what God gave you. Another opportunity to love and be loved. Take it from me, that's hard to come by."

"Yeah, well, you'll find someone."

"That's why I need to get you married off. Then I can be the Cole brother all the women are after."

Grayson threw his head back and laughed. "It's not as great as it sounds."

"So you say." Bronson shook his head and looked past Grayson toward the ranch. "Let's get home. Ma will be excited about Nora coming tomorrow."

"Yeah, you go on ahead. I'm gonna go see Sophia."

His brother searched his face for a sign of what Grayson felt. He must have seen what he needed because his shoulders relaxed. "Tell her hello for me."

When Grayson reached the family graveyard, he dismounted and considered if he should pluck some wildflowers. He froze when looking across the patch of land toward Sophia's grave. The entire area was covered in blue flowers; hundreds of them in soft patterns resembling waves.

Grayson could only smile. "I see you've been decorating, Sophia. They're beautiful."

The breeze blew across, moving the flowers in accord, as if they preened at his compliment. Grayson removed his hat and sank to the ground next to Sophia's headstone. "I met someone. I think you'd like her..."

He choked when the breeze made the wildflowers sway. "I can't do it Sophia. I can't do it." The familiar constriction in his chest came so fast he almost fell over. "God Sophia, how can I even consider another woman? I—I don't think I can do it. I'm fooling myself, aren't I?"

Once again the wildflowers swayed, this time the wind picked up, as if angry at his words. He watched the flowers not sure what to think.

Finally, he gave in to the sadness and leaned across her grave. "Losing you hurt so bad, Sophia. I can't do go through it again." Tears plopped onto the ground. "I'll have to let Nora go."

"Your Ma sent me to come check on you," Hank Cole said. He walked past Grayson, who now sat on a fallen tree, to stand next to the cross marking Sophia's grave. "You know how she is about you, boy."

"Sakes, Pa, I'm not a five year old that gets lost," Grayson snapped back. Truth be told, he was more irritated with himself for making his mother worry than anything else.

His father ignored the outburst. "Well, I did my part." He pulled out his tobacco pouch and proceeded to roll a cigarette. "Bronson says you're bringing Nora for supper tomorrow evening."

Each time he considered his plans the next day with Nora, his stomach tied into knots. "I'm not sure, now." Shoving his hands deep into his pockets, Grayson looked directly at his father. "I just can't."

For a second, Hank Cole met his stare. Hank's nod was slow. "I see. If you're not ready to move on, then you're not ready. Can't nothing be done about that. It's a shame about Nora, I like that spitfire of a gal." He looked to Sophia's marker once again. "No offense to

Sophia, but she was a meek one. You could come and go as you pleased and she never had the backbone to stand up to you."

Grayson had to agree. "Yeah, she did allow me plenty of freedom."

"You know," Hank began, watching the smoke from his cigarette swirl. "If you have no intentions of marrying Nora Banks, you owe it to her to let her go. She's a pretty one and will make someone a good wife." He scratched his chin. "I wonder if she and Ashley maybe could get to know each other."

Grayson's eyes bulged. "Ashley?"

"Why not?" Walking in a circle now, Hank nodded, his eyes downward. "He needs to settle down, quit with all the moping about. A strong woman like that would be good for him."

"Pa, you expect me to tell her I'm not interested and then offer up my brother?" It was difficult to swallow past his suddenly dry throat. "I won't do that. I can't see her with Ashley."

"What about Bronson?"

"No, Pa." Grayson huffed. "It would be easier for me if she wasn't around here."

"So you care for her then?"

Grayson pushed at the dirt with the toe of his boot. "Yeah, I do."

"Then you want her to be happy. Son, the girl's reputation is going to be in tatters. Already the townsfolk had a field day over the instance at the barn. Now she's going to find herself without a fiancé."

"Her father didn't seem to have any compunction over it, coming here to break the engagement when Ashley was in jail." Grayson mimicked his father and began walking in a slow circle. "What do you expect me to do?"

"Arthur Banks was Carolyn's puppet. Hate to speak ill of the dead, but that's the truth. As for you, for starters, I expect you to be a man of your word, Gray. But if you are not going to follow through with this, then I suggest we find her someone who'll stand in for you."

Grayson took his hat off and jerked his fingers through his hair. He glanced at his father hoping to find the answer in the face too much like his own. "Damn it, Pa, can't this wait."

"No it cannot. I understand you went through a loss and you know what? There are going to be more. Your Ma and I are gonna die. One of your brothers may die before you. Death is part of life, son. Accept it."

The stark truth slapped him like an icy wind and took his breath. Hank neared until they were almost nose-to-nose. "I am not downplaying your pain of losing your wife so soon after getting married, but, son, it's been long enough. Ultimately, it's your decision. If you're going to back out of marrying Nora, talk to her. I'm sure she'd rather be alone than with a husband that doesn't want to be married."

"Yes, sir."

"Come on now, it's almost supper time."

They walked back together, Grayson pulling his horse along. Thankfully, his father allowed him time to sort out his thoughts. By the time he arrived at the ranch, his mind was made up. Problem was, how he was going to tell her.

Chapter Twenty

"Ouch!" Nora put her burned finger in her mouth. "The pie tins are still hot," she told her brother who sat at the kitchen table eating lunch.

"What did you expect? You just took them out of the oven." His remark annoyed her and she rolled her eyes at him.

"I wanted to put them closer to the window to let them cool." She frowned down at her brother. "This is a bad idea. I should just hand Grayson a darn pie and tell him to take it as an apology for me not going with him to dinner."

Her statement met silence. Mitch had gone back to reading the newspaper in the middle of her statement. Just as well, there was nothing he could say on the matter that would make any difference to the jumble of emotions tumbling through her since Grayson left the day before. One minute she was giddy and excited, the next terrified. Surely, after he'd gone on his way and his blood cooled, he'd realize what a bad suggestion he'd made in the heat of the moment.

"I'm going upstairs to change, please don't touch the pies." She tapped his shoulder and Mitch looked up at her.

"What?"

"Don't. Touch. Pies," She growled and hurried from the room.

"I thought one was for us," he called after her.

On the second floor, Nora walked down the hallway. Her mother's door was open and she glanced in. Carolyn Banks sat at her dressing table. She held something in her hands and stared blankly out the window. "Mama?"

"Oh, hello, dear," her mother said as she turned toward the door and Nora was relieved to see her face was tear free. "I was just thinking about you."

Puzzled, Nora entered and moved closer. "About me?"

"Why yes. I've decided that perhaps we should go to Virginia. Visit my sister there and present you to polite society. You're not going to find a suitable husband here and it's time I think of others besides myself. Once you get settled, then Mitch can do the same here. Or come with us if he pleases. We can sell the mercantile. Your father provided well for us."

"What about you? Where do you plan to live?"

Carolyn Banks held out a letter she held. "Your Aunt Martha has invited me to come, to move to Virginia. She is widowed as well and I'm considering it." Her eyes twinkled at Nora. "Oh, to live in the city again. You have no idea how dreadful it's been living so far from all the comforts."

Nora sat on the trunk at the foot of her parents' bed. "I had no idea you felt that way, Mother."

Carolyn sighed and offered a soft smile. "I did it for your father. It was his dream to come here. To start a business of his own, just like his father did in Virginia. He was quite the dreamer, your father."

A dreamer? Nora had a hard time picturing the young Arthur Banks and even less success thinking about him being a young dreamer. Her father's only goal in life seemed to be doting on her mother, always at her beck and call. He never acted as if it bothered him.

"Father was a good man."

"Yes, he was," her mother agreed. "And I took him for

granted." She sniffed. Nora's eyes widened, not so much at her mother's tears, but at the statement. "All he did was try to make me happy to ensure I didn't complain about living out here."

"He loved you, Mama. I don't think he minded."

A soft smile curved her mother's lips. "Every once in a while, he'd get annoyed with me. In his own quiet way, Arthur would let me know his displeasure at whatever it was I asked of him." Carolyn shook her head at a memory. "After he'd fetched me coffee one time, he placed the cup down and walked away. I went to drink from it and it was empty." She chuckled. "When I asked him why he brought me an empty cup, he said, 'I asked you for an apple pie for dessert and that's what I got'."

Nora laughed. "That does sound like something he'd do." She reached and patted her mother's hand. "When are you planning this trip east?"

"It depends on what Mitch wants to do," her mother replied. "If he's keeping the house and the mercantile, then I'll leave more things behind and it will be sooner." She looked about the room assessing. "Although we probably will have to sell most everything."

Grayson would be there any minute and this turn of events had Nora wondering what to say. "I'm going to supper at the Coles' tonight. You do remember?"

"Ah, yes. Goodness, Nora, it's best you break things off and the sooner the better. Out east, no one will know of all this unfortunate mess between the two of you. Grayson Cole is not the marrying kind, mark my words."

Not one to allow others to think for her, Nora met her mother's eyes. "I will decide my future, Mother. Whether or not I move east and what happens between Grayson and me. I don't foresee marrying him, because he may not be inclined to marry, but it's a decision that he and I must make together."

Once again, her mother surprised her and lifted her eyebrows in approval. "Very well. But I will not leave you behind unless you are married and both you and I know that's hardly possible if you've got your heart set on that Cole boy. So think on it and make up your mind soon."

The ride out to the Cole ranch was mired in awkward silence. Grayson replied to her questions with clipped one or two word answers until she gave up attempting to hold a conversation. He slowed the horses when they reached the outskirts of the Cole lands and she took the opportunity to speak again.

"Can we stop for a minute? I need to talk to you."

Grayson's eyes slid from her toward his house and he swallowed visibly. "I suppose we can."

Nora glared at him. "Why do I get the feeling that you'd rather be anywhere but here with me right now?"

His brows came together and he pressed his lips into a tight line before letting out a breath. "I have a lot on my mind, it's that..." He scratched at his jaw, the stubble on his cheek making a soft rasp. "Damn it, Nora, just give me a minute."

"I haven't done anything. I'm just sitting here," Nora said and crossed her arms. "Take me home," she snapped.

With fluid movements at odds with his large size, Grayson climbed down from the wagon and rounded it. He held his hand up to her. "Come, please."

She frowned at his outstretched hand before taking it. This was it. He would tell her how sorry he was for leading her on and that he needed her to understand he wasn't going to settle down. Of course, he'd attempt to sooth her feelings with promises of lingering thoughts of her. Soft promises that would not mean much.

Nora walked alongside him, her hand in his. As much as she wanted to snatch it away, at the same time, touching him one last time felt good. His large hand enveloping hers gave her strength. No matter what he said, she'd accept it with grace and as much dignity as she could muster.

Blue aster covered the field where they came to a stop. She admired the waves of the varying shades of blue, a stark reminder of how Grayson's eyes changed color according to his moods. When he turned to her, they were bright, brighter than she'd ever seen them. "Lots of flowers here, aren't there?' His question was easy enough to answer.

"It's blue aster. I don't think I've ever seen a more beautiful display." Nora released his hand and took a couple steps forward, the entire time looking over the field. Her eyes stopped on several grave markers, the sturdy crosses lording over the field of blue. "Is this your family's cemetery?"

Grayson nodded with his gaze on her. "Yes, my grandmother is over there." He pointed to a marker on the far left of a set of four. "Next to her is my grandpa, Hank."

The breeze picked up and the display of blue shifted easily. For some reason, tears sprung and Nora looked away from Grayson. "Sophia is here, too?"

"Yes," his quiet reply held huskiness to it. "She is the last marker on the right, next to my brother, Joseph."

"I didn't know you had another brother." Nora scanned the markers, but they were too far in the distance to read clearly.

"He died when he was an infant. He'd be younger than Bronson and me."

"Is this why you hesitated to stop when I asked you?" Nora asked, noting he'd moved closer and now stood at her side. His hand moved to the small of her back.

"No. Not at all. If anything, it's a good place for us to talk. I find it peaceful here."

This was it. Nora swallowed. "Look, Grayson, I know you are attempting to find a way to take back what you said at my mother's house. I understand little about passion, but enough to know that at those times, things are said that feel right at that moment."

"Is that what you think?" The confused expression made her want to slap him. The infuriating man was ruining her attempt to let him off easy.

"Of course," she replied. "What else would you have to say to me?"

He took her by the shoulders and turned her to face him. "I have plenty to say to you, Nora. I want you to know that you scare me. You've made me lose interest in other women. I even drank because of you, something I'm not good at. I'm constantly torn between getting away from you and wanting to be with you."

"I'm not sure I'm flattered by all that." Nora frowned up at him only to have his mouth over hers stopping whatever she was going to say.

The gentle kiss took her breath and she leaned in to him allowing his arms to circle her in a warm embrace. *Sophia's grave.* Nora pushed away from Grayson, her eyes wide.

"What's wrong?" Grayson asked not reaching for her.

"It—it doesn't feel right to be kissing here, in front of your wife." She didn't dare to look toward the grave.

Grayson's lips curved and he looked down at his feet. "I told her about you."

"You did?"

"Yep, that same day, the one you claim I was over-passioned." He smiled widely at her. "I was confused and scared."

"Of what?" She neared and his arms automatically went around her.

"Of the pain that comes from choosing between losing someone you love and allowing them to get so close you can't imagine life without them."

Nora trembled.

"Nora." Grayson's arms slipped from around her and he kneeled. He took his hat off allowing it to fall to the ground and looked up at her, taking her hands. "I am in love with you, I know I haven't made it easy for you to trust me, but at this moment, I promise you that I'm only yours for the rest of my life, if you will have me."

For the first time, she knew what this bright shade of blue in his eyes meant. It was love and Nora's heart pounded so hard, she wasn't sure it wasn't an affliction. Her breathing hitched as she looked down at the man of her dreams.

"Marry me, Nora."

"Oh God, yes!" She pulled him up to stand and threw herself against the expanse of his chest. "Yes! Yes! Yes!"

"I take that as a yes." Grayson's laughter rang across the field and the blue asters seemed to agree, waving gaily in return.

Nora's sharp intake of breath made Grayson's expression harden. "What is it?"

"There's something you need to know about me."

"All right, but I'm not going to let you out of marrying me. Come, let's sit." He guided her to a fallen tree.

The happiness of the moment left her and she knew that once she divulged her secret, Grayson would bow out of the proposal. Why had she said yes? Why had she allowed herself to even for a moment think she could have a life with him?

Her hands trembled and Grayson reached for them. She stepped back. Her eyes rounded and she put a hand over her mouth. Tears threatened at the knowledge she was about to lose the only man she ever loved.

"I can't marry you, Grayson." He started to speak and she lifted her hand to stop him. "Listen to me. It is you who will not want to marry me once I tell you this. You won't want to be with someone like me."

"Talk to me." His eyes bore into hers.

Nora swallowed down the bile that rose into her throat. "You know you were not my first...er..."

"Lover?" he supplied.

"You are my first lover, but not my first *experience*."

Nora forged ahead before losing her nerve. "The first time was with the man, the stranger I shot."

"So you knew him then?" His expression was guarded, not telling her what he thought.

"Yes, in a way I did. He took my virginity. It was not consensual."

What resembled a groan came from Grayson. "What happened?"

He took a step back, the wall lifting between them already. Even if she wanted to stop now, she couldn't. He had a right to know.

"I was fifteen, Mitch sixteen. We were returning from a hayride and stopped when we saw the man on the side of the road. He acted as if he needed help. He knocked Mitch unconscious and dragged me into the woods, to that shack. Once inside, he...he took me. Hit me when I tried to get away and threatened to kill Mitch if I didn't do what he said. It was several hours before he let me go and find my barely conscious brother."

"If I would have known, I would have killed him myself." A muscle on Grayson's jawline jerked. "I'm sorry that happened to you, Nora."

He moved closer, but didn't touch her. Not wanting to see the distaste or pity in his eyes, she kept hers trained on the ground between them. "I know most men won't want to marry someone who's been raped."

"How can you be so strong?" His voice was hoarse, hesitant, as if he didn't quite know how to accept what she said.

"I've let it go slowly. I had to in order to move on. It happened and I have dealt with it. I needed you to know. And if you can't accept it, I understand."

"I admire you and what you've just shared does nothing to change that. It also has no bearing on how much I love you." Grayson kissed her again. She ran her fingers into his hair, not wanting to let him go.

Time stopped as she became lost in his kisses. Finally,

Grayson pressed his forehead to hers. "We should go."

"Oh God, Grayson, we're going to be late for supper." Nora set to adjusting her dress and then straightening her hair. "Oh no, look what you did." She pulled pins from her now lopsided bun and the golden brown waves fell to her waist.

Instead of looking apologetic, he seemed more proud, with a crooked grin on his face. "I can't wait to see you like that every night." Grayson winked and moved toward her.

Nora attempted to glare at him. "Stop right there, Grayson Cole." She held her arms out, her palms facing him. "Don't come near me, right now."

"I hope you won't be saying that after we're married."

Her lips curved. "Never."

Epilogue

Nora sniffed against Grayson's chest as the train pulled away from the station. The sounds of its whistle still a new sound in the region. Her mother left for Virginia alone, satisfied that Nora, now happily married, did not need her. Mitch had decided he'd remain.

"We can visit her once the house is built," Grayson soothed, rubbing her back. "Besides, I'm sure once we have babies, she'll come often."

"Babies?" The word took Nora's mind from her angst.

"Of course," Grayson replied, "with all the practicing we've been doing, it won't be long."

Nora gasped and searched the people nearby to ensure no one overhead. "Hush now, Grayson, goodness you can't talk like that in public."

He ignored her and gave her a wide smile. "Come along, Missus Cole, we've got to get back to town. You're going to help Mitch at the store and I better get back over to the land and see how the team is doing with the construction. Just a couple more weeks and we'll move in and then Mitch can have your parents' house."

She snuggled into his side. "He doesn't mind living above the mercantile. But you're right. As soon as he gets settled in the house, it will be time for him to set his mind on finding a suitable wife."

"I have a feeling you plan to help with that." Grayson took her elbow and steered her from the platform.

"I do," she admitted. "Mitch deserves a wife and family. He's spent his entire life looking after me. But now that I have a new, handsome protector, he is free." Her eyes twinkled up at him.

"I love you, Nora."

"I know you do, Grayson. There isn't one single doubt in my mind."

The couple kissed, not caring who passed by.

The End

From the Author

Dear Reader,

Hope you enjoyed *A Different Shade of Blue,* please recommend it to your friends and family. Remember, reviews are like candy to authors. We love them.

I love hearing from my readers and am always excited when you join my newsletter to keep abreast of new releases and other things happening in my world. Newsletter sign up: http://goo.gl/PH6Doo

Other Hildie McQueen Links:

Website: http://www.HildieMcQueen.com

Facebook: http://www.facebook.com/HildieMcQueen

Twitter: https://twitter.com/HildieMcQueen

Instagram: @HildieWrites

I answer all emails: Hildie@HildieMcQueen.com

HILDIE McQUEEN
ENTICING. ENGAGING. ROMANCE.